CHINA'S LONG MARCH

Jean Fritz

CHINA'S LONG MARCH
6,000 Miles of Danger

With Illustrations by Yang Zhr Cheng

G. P. PUTNAM'S SONS, NEW YORK

ACKNOWLEDGMENTS

I am deeply indebted to the people who have made it possible for me to do the research for this book. To Li Weihe and Xu Jiaxian of the Embassy of the People's Republic of China in Washington, D.C., who found a sponsor for me and made it possible for me to visit China. To all the members of the Chinese Association for International Understanding who went to extraordinary lengths to arrange my itinerary and interviews with survivors of the Long March. Their friendship, kindness, and interest in my project were unwavering.

Finally I want to thank John Bryan Starr, Executive Director of the Yale-China Association, for his generosity in checking my manuscript.

G. P. Putnam's Sons, a division of
Penguin Putnam Books for Young Readers.
345 Hudson Street, New York, NY 10014.
Printed in the United States of America.
Book designed by Gunta Alexander.
Maps by Jeanyee Wong.

Library of Congress Catalogue-in-Publication Data
Fritz, Jean.   China's Long March : 6,000 miles of danger/
Jean Fritz : with illustrations by Yang Zhr Cheng.
p. cm. Bibliography: p.   Summary: Describes the events of
the 6,000 mile march undertaken by Mao Zedong and his
Communist followers as they retreated before the forces of
Chiang Kai-shek. 1. China—History—Long March, 1934-1935
—Juvenile literature. [1. China—History—Long March,
1934-1935.]   I. ____,___, ill. II. Title.
DS777.5134.F74 1988 951.04'2—dc19 87-311171   CIP   AC
ISBN 0-399-21512-3
10 9 8 7 6 5

TO KUO-HO AND IRENE CHANG

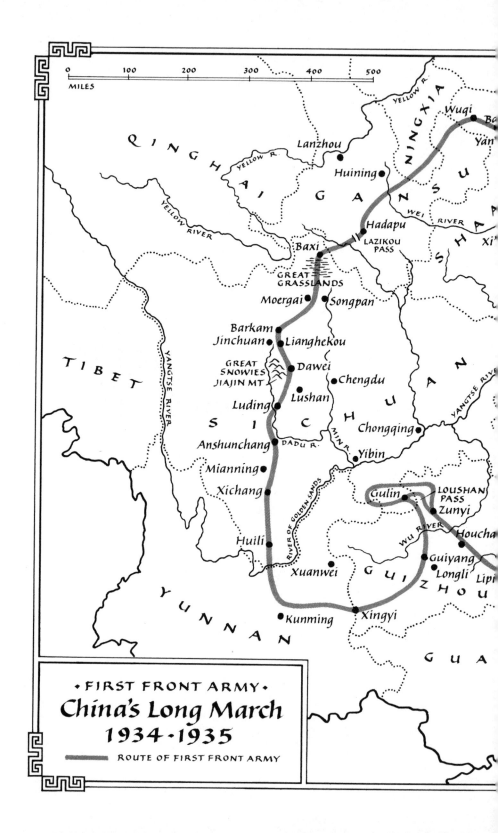

MILES

QINGHAI

Lanzhou

GANSU

NINGXIA

Wuqi

Ba

Yan'

YELLOW R.

Huining

YELLOW R.

YELLOW RIVER

WEI RIVER

Hadapu

Xi

Baxi

LAZIKOU PASS

GREAT GRASSLANDS

Moergai

Songpan

SHAANXI

Barkam

Jinchuan

Lianghekou

TIBET

YANGTSE RIVER

GREAT SNOWIES JIAJIN MT

Dawei

Chengdu

Luding

Lushan

SICHUAN

YANGTSE RIVER

Anshunchang

DADU R.

Chongqing

Mianning

MIN R.

Yibin

Xichang

RIVER OF GOLDEN SANDS

Gulin

LOUSHAN PASS

Zunyi

WU RIVER

Houcha

Huili

Guiyang

Xuanwei

GUIZHOU

Longli

Lipi

YUNNAN

Kunming

Xingyi

GUA

· FIRST FRONT ARMY ·
China's Long March
1934·1935

ROUTE OF FIRST FRONT ARMY

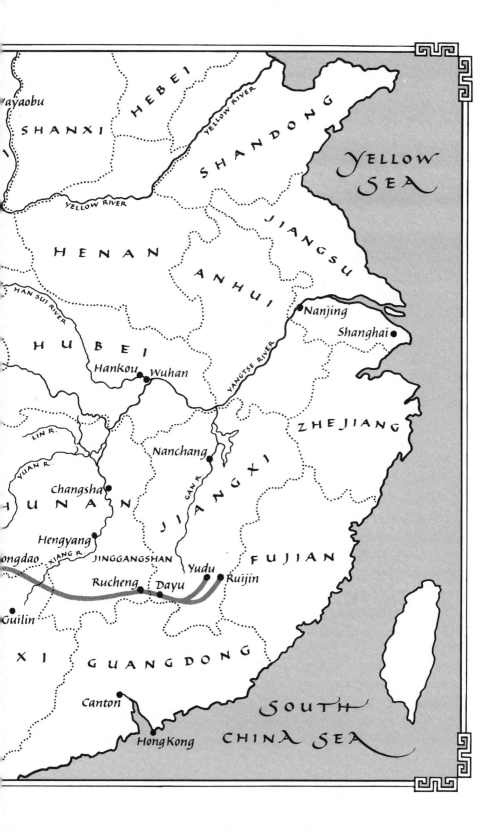

ayaobu

SHANXI

HEBEI

SHANDONG

YELLOW RIVER

YELLOW SEA

JIANGSU

HENAN

YELLOW RIVER

ANHUI

HAN SUI RIVER

HUBEI

Hankou Wuhan

Nanjing

Shanghai

YANGTSE RIVER

ZHEJIANG

LIN R.

Nanchang

YUAN R.

Changsha

JIANGXI

HUNAN

GAN R.

Hengyang

FUJIAN

ongdao

XIANG R.

JINGGANGSHAN

Yudu

Rucheng

Dayu

Ruijin

Guilin

XI

GUANGDONG

Canton

SOUTH

Hong Kong

CHINA SEA

A NOTE ON PRONUNCIATION

In most cases I have used the pinyin system for spelling Chinese words and names. This system was officially adopted by the People's Republic of China in 1958. The main points to remember are: *q* is used for the *ch* sound; *x* is used for *sh* except that it has a slight hiss to the sound so it can be represented as *hs*; *zh* is for *j*; and *c* for *ts* as in *its*.

A guide to the pronunciation of some of the more common names and words used in this book may be helpful.

Chen Changfeng	Chen chahng-fung
Chiang Kai-shek	Jiahng kigh-shek
Kang Keqing	Kahng kuh-ching
Li Xiauxia	Lee hsee-ow-hsah
Lin Biao	Lin bee-ow
Liu Ying	Li-oo ying
Mao Zedong	Mow (as in *how*) dzuh-doong
Yang Chengwu	Yahng chung-woo
Zhang Guotao	Jahng gwo-tow (as in *how*)
Zhou Enlai	Joe en-lye
Zhu De	Jew duh
Jiangxi	Jiahng hsi
Sichuan	Tse chwan
Xiang	Hsiahng
Zunyi	Tswun yee

BEFORE THE LONG MARCH

The Chinese are proud of their Long March, that incredible 6,000-mile, year-long epic of escape and survival made by the young Communist Army in 1934 to 1935. Today museums stand at important points along the route. On school playgrounds children play at being heroes and heroines as they cross miniature mountains and make-believe rivers—obstacle courses made to represent the path of the March. If you talk to survivors of the March, as I did in the spring of 1986, you will see their faces light up as they recount their memories. For in spite of (and perhaps because of) unspeakable hardships, this year of close comradeship and of shared idealism was a high point in their lives as well as in their revolution.

But what brought about a revolution in the first place? Poverty, for one thing. Injustice. Hundreds and hundreds of years of it. Foreigners who came to China and took unfair advantage of the Chinese. And finally the emperors and empresses who ruled China. They lived in splendor and took little interest in the welfare of the common people.

In 1905 a man named Sun Yat-sen, one of the many who knew that China could not go on like this, started an organization dedicated to reform. If only the people could get rid of the imperial system with its emperors and empresses, then they could change China. By 1911 they had raised an army and did manage to overthrow the last imperial dynasty of China. Still, they didn't have enough power or enough money to change China or even to rule it.

11

So who would rule now? Warlords tried. They conquered pieces of territory and fought other warlords for more territory. Sun Yat-sen tried to strengthen his party (known now as the Nationalist Party) and eventually, in 1924, because he couldn't find any other outside help, he accepted the help of Communist Russia which, having completed a revolution of its own, was eager to spread revolution to other countries. In 1921, however, a small group of Chinese had already formed a Chinese Communist Party, but since their first goal was to unify the country, they were willing to work within the Nationalist Party. The Nationalists, who needed all the help they could get, accepted them.

Then in 1925 Sun Yat-sen died and the following year General Chiang Kai-shek became the leader of the Nationalists and gradually it became clear that the Nationalists and the Communists were not getting along. The Nationalists held conservative views about the future of China, talking mainly about unifying the nation and making it independent of foreign domination. But the Communists talked of turning Chinese society upside down so life would be better for poor people, especially the peasants who made up eighty percent of the population. More and more Chiang Kai-shek felt threatened by the growing strength of the Communists, so in 1927 he not only threw them out of the Party (along with his Russian advisors) but began executing Communists wherever he could find them. From that time the Nationalists and the Communists were enemies.

This story opens in 1934. By this time Chiang Kai-shek's Nationalist regime was recognized by most foreign countries as the legal government of China. But not by the Communists. In the interior of China they were building up their army and spreading their revolution among the peasants. They were still determined to make over China.

The scene is Jiangxi, a remote mountainous province in southern China. The danger is about to begin.

ONE  Something was going to happen. The soldiers knew it; the peasants suspected it. Whatever was coming, it was more than just another battle. Ever since 1927, when the first scattered segments of the Communist Army had moved into Jiangxi Province, there had been battles— small skirmishes at first. Then in 1930 the Nationalist Army began forming a circle around the Communists as if they meant to squeeze the life right out of them. Fighting behind concrete blockhouses strung together with barbed wire, the Nationalists had now drawn the circle so close they were able to keep all goods from entering it. The Communist soldiers and the peasants laughed at the blockhouses, calling them "tortoises," but they needed those goods, so they knew the tortoises had to be stopped. Three times in the past they had stopped them. Quick, sharp jabs at the en-

13

emy. Surprise moves. And each time the Communist troops had returned with stores of captured weapons and long lines of captured soldiers. But not the fourth and last time. In April 1934 the Communist or Red Army (as it was called) met with disaster. Four thousand men were killed; 20,000 were captured and sixty counties fell into enemy hands.

So of course there would be battles, but something more lay ahead now. Otherwise, why were the peasants told to make the straw sandals for the soldiers thicker than usual? And why the jackets heavier? The fighting was here in Jiangxi Province, where it was still warm. Wherever the soldiers fought, they would surely come back. This was their home base and for many Jiangxi was also their home. The peasants who had sons or fathers in the army hung red banners down their front doors. From one family alone eight brothers had joined up and of course they were envied, for most people in this area were true revolutionaries and were proud to make sacrifices.

After all, they knew how lucky they were to have an army fighting for them and how important it was for this army to win. Like peasants all over China, they had been so poor for so long, they took for granted that they'd always be poor. The landlords who owned most of the ground they farmed would just go on taking their money, whether they had it or not. Many times they didn't have it. If it rained too much and the crops failed or if it didn't rain enough, still the landlords demanded half their harvest and taxes were often figured years in advance. A peasant could knock his head on the floor and beg his landlord for mercy but not many landlords had much mercy in them. So the peasant would have to give up his land and in effect become the landlord's slave. One young peasant boy often wondered how landlords could have such normal, ordinary-looking faces and yet be so cruel. How could the cruelty not show?

Moreover, it was not only landlords but also warlords who

taxed peasants while their armies marched through the countryside, stealing their pigs and chickens, plundering their fields. And what could the peasants do? Only what they'd always done. Pray to the gods for protection and paste pictures of warrior gods on their front doors to frighten away evil spirits. It was no wonder that the peasants called themselves "dry people"—those who had been sucked dry of everything.

At first when the Red Army had moved here, the peasants had shooed their pigs and chickens into their little dirt-floored huts and banged their doors shut. This was just another thieving army, they supposed, and it took them a while to understand that this army was different. They didn't steal from the poor. Instead they put up signs: DOWN WITH THE RICH! UP WITH THE POOR! LEARN, LEARN, LEARN AGAIN! STUDY WHILE YOU PLOW! Best of all, they took land away from the landlords and gave it to the peasants. For the first time the poor people of Jiangxi Province felt that they no longer had to go through life cringing. They had a *right* to live.

And they were willing to fight for that right. But what was the army planning? they asked each other. Rumors kindled and spread like grassfire throughout the province. Certainly the one hundred men who had been hired to climb the fortresslike mountain of Jinggangshan in the spring of 1934 must have talked. Their empty baskets swinging lightly at each end of their carrying poles, they had climbed this mountain to a hidden cave where their baskets had been filled with bundles so heavy that the men must have guessed that this was money. One hundred million silver dollars— that's what they were taking back to Army Headquarters. But how could poor peasants have imagined so much money dangling from their shoulders?

Whatever the army was planning, it needed not only money but men. After their spring losses, the army had to be replenished, but did it also have to pack up everything it owned? As summer wore into fall, people could see the preparations that were being made and their hearts sank. Just look at the equipment that was being amassed! Medicine, guns, cannon, radios, telephones, telephone wires, books, chests of documents. No matter how heavy the equipment, it was included: printing presses, engraving plates for printing money, X-ray machines, office furniture and files, sewing machines. And see what else was there! Scenery for dramatic performances. Costumes. The army was used to putting on plays for soldiers and villagers, so why were they taking their theatrical materials away? Certainly they were not planning to entertain the enemy. No, it was clear that the army was moving out. They were withdrawing, leaving Jiangxi Province.

The peasants knew what that meant. Once the army had left, the Nationalists would move in. They'd give the land back to the landlords and kill all those whom they suspected of having helped the Communists. Even when the peasants were told that some army units would be left behind to protect them, they were not convinced. How could a few units hold the Nationalists back when so many units had not been able to do so? They shook their heads. No, the old days would be back. Even worse than before.

The soldiers had their own worries. If only their old leaders, Mao Zedong and Zhu De, were still in command, they would have had more confidence in what was coming. Mao Zedong, in charge of political decisions, and Zhu De, in charge of military matters, worked so well together that they had become known as Zhu-Mao, as if they were just one man. They had done well too. After all, they had defeated the enemy in those first three encirclement campaigns.

But Mao Zedong and Zhu De were no longer planning the strategy. Now the man in charge was a German, Otto Braun, sent by the Communist Party headquarters in Shanghai and in turn sent by the Russians who, though thrown out by the Nationalists, were still helping the Communists. But who

16

among the soldiers could trust Otto Braun? What did he know about China? He didn't speak Chinese, wouldn't eat rice or drink tea, and to the Chinese he looked like a caricature of a foreigner. Tall, blue-eyed, not only did he have a big nose as all foreigners did (Chinese call foreigners "Big Noses") but he had a nose so big that sometimes he covered it with a handkerchief, as if he could fool the Chinese into thinking that he was one of them. Most serious, according to Mao, he didn't know how to fight against a superior force. He wasn't interested in trying to surprise or outwit the enemy. Mao's guerrilla tactics, Braun said, were out of date. But as everyone remembered—soldiers and officers alike—it was Otto Braun who had been in command in April when they had suffered that terrible defeat.

So both the soldiers and the peasants were dispirited as the time drew near for the army to move out. Still, no matter what lay ahead, the peasants had to say good-bye and good luck to their soldiers. From all over the province the villagers came to Army Headquarters with gifts of eggs, knitted socks, and whatever treats they could find. It was hard to part. Many fathers begged their sons to stay. Many sons who had never been out of the province suddenly couldn't bear to think about the strange places and lonely nights that lay ahead. Twenty-year-old Yang Chengwu, an experienced Communist and soon to be a political commissar, met his father and his friends, who had walked forty miles to bring him rabbits and dried sweet potatoes. Looking at these people who were so dear to him, he was overwhelmed with a sense of homesickness. How could he leave this beloved countryside of his childhood?

"Go," his father said. "If you remain here, you'll be killed."

On October 15 the army began to leave, but it was several days before they were all out. There were 86,000 men, 30 women, 676 horses, and 5,000 porters hired to carry the heavy equipment. It was a young army. More than half the men were between sixteen and twenty-three, and in addition there were several hundred teenagers known affectionately as "little red devils." They were the buglers of the army and would become the water carriers, firewood gatherers, cooks' helpers, and messengers.

As they started out, each soldier had, in addition to his rifle and ammunition, a ten-day supply of rice which he carried in a banana-shaped bag around his neck. In his knapsack were a blanket, a change of clothes, comb, brush, notebook, and soap. Strapped to his belt was a big enamel cup with a toothbrush and towel stuffed into it. A pair of chopsticks was thrust into his leg wrappings, or puttees, while a threaded needle was stuck under the peak of his red-starred cap, covered now with leaves to serve as camouflage. And because he was a soldier in the Red Army, a piece of red yarn was woven somewhere into one of his straw sandals. One man wore a pair of sandals on which an enthusiastic peasant had embroidered the words "Kill the Invaders!"

But where were they going? Otto Braun, who supposedly knew the answer, did not believe in confiding in soldiers. They were meant to obey, he said, not ask questions. But the soldiers made guesses. While they were members of the First Front Army (the main army), there were other Communist armies stationed elsewhere. Perhaps they were going to join the Second Front Army in northern Hunan Province. Perhaps they were heading for the Fourth Front Army in Sichuan Province. The more optimistic ones said they were just going to capture a city and would then come home. Some thought they would march only a week or two and then settle down in a new base.

Mao Zedong and Zhu De, however, were well aware that not even Otto Braun knew where they were going. They would surely start toward Hunan, but who could be certain where they would end up? They simply had to escape from the enemy. No one knew how long they'd be on the road or how far they would have to travel.

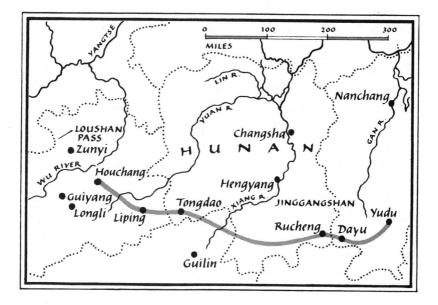

TWO Long before the army started, scouts had been sneaking into enemy territory to spy out enemy positions. As usual, Scout Kong was in the lead. There was nothing Kong liked better than to be in the thick of danger. In battle his voice would be heard above all others. *"Sha!"* he would cry—Kill! *"Sha! Sha!"* But of course as a scout he had to be silent and sly, hiding sometimes for hours in the top branches of a tree, watching enemy movements, estimating enemy strength. He knew all the tricks to use if he was caught. "Act dumb," Zhu De had told him. "Pretend to be a traveling ear-cleaner." Since Chinese loved to have their ears cleaned, there were many professional ear-cleaners who went about with their tiny bamboo cleaning instruments. No one would be suspicious of an ear-cleaner. Or if Kong had a message to deliver, Zhu De said, he should pretend to be a farmer. Write the message on rice paper and hide it in a basket of vegetables.

So far, Scout Kong hadn't needed to resort to these tricks and over the summer he'd returned again and again from the enemy lines with good news. The enemy was taking it easy, Kong reported. Many troops had been withdrawn; none seemed to be on the alert for action. Apparently Chiang Kai-shek had decided that the Red Army was not only trapped but so outnumbered there was no need to worry. Besides, Chiang had another source of trouble on his hands. Japan was attacking China in the north, and once the Communist threat was over he could give his attention to the Japanese. In any case, Kong said, there were weak spots in the enemy barricade which, with luck, might be penetrated.

Nevertheless, they took no chances. The army left at night, traveled at night, and rested in the day under camphor trees and alders, out of sight as much as possible. Their first obstacle was the Yudu River but it was shallow and narrow. They rattled over the five pontoons that had been thrown across the river and many soldiers simply waded to the other side. Later the army would dread the rivers that lay in their path, but who could foresee that now? No one was thinking of their march in terms of the whole map of China, with its two parent rivers, the Yangtse River and the Yellow River, and all their tributaries spilling across the country like children running away from home.

From end to end the army stretched for sixty miles as it snaked single-file over mountain trails so narrow that the men wore white kerchiefs on their backs to guide those behind them. On rainy nights when the paths became slippery, they had to be especially careful. One misstep could send a man crashing over the side of a cliff. Or a group of men might go together, leaving behind a gap and a silence where they had just been.

But there were good times as well. On a moonlit night a

group of men would start to sing and their song would be picked up by another group farther down the line, then again by another, their voices unrolling like a ribbon under the stars. At times like this they all felt warmed by their brotherhood in the revolution, for, though many of the leaders were educated, at heart this was a peasant army, fighting for the peasants of China.

Zhu De himself, who at forty-eight was one of the oldest of the army, had grown up in a peasant family under a landlord so brutal that he was known to his tenants as the King of Hell. As a child Zhu De had never had enough to eat, often not even rice but only a gruel made from a kind of corn fodder. As the family grew, food became scarcer and scarcer, and when there were seven children, Zhu's parents knew they simply could not feed another mouth. To keep them all from starving, his parents drowned their last five children at birth.

Zhu De's wife, Kang Keqing, not only came from a peasant family but also had the bad luck to be born a girl. Every girl from a poor family was a disappointment, hardly worth the trouble of raising since in the end a girl went to live and work in her husband's home while a boy brought his wife home to his parents. Kang Keqing hated so much being a girl that on the night before her wedding she ran away from a marriage that had been arranged for her, from a wedding she didn't want, from a husband she didn't know. At the same time she was running away from being a woman in a society in which women counted for nothing. She joined the Red Army.

And here she was now, a combat soldier! She wasn't marching in the group with the other women; instead she was swinging along with other combat soldiers, a rifle on her shoulder. Like all Communist women, she had cut her hair to show that she was liberated, and when she married Zhu De two years after joining the army, she made it clear that his bodyguards could do the cooking and the sewing. She was through with women's work.

They had common roots, these soldiers, and up and down that long line each one had his or her own story. Somewhere in that line, for instance, was a little red devil who had been twelve years old when he first went to the recruiting office. He said he was thirteen but when he was asked why he wanted to join, he couldn't find any words. How could he tell a recruiting officer that he was an orphan and worked for a cruel landlord? Was that a reason? He hung his head. "I don't know," he said, so he was rejected.

A few months later the boy went back and said he was fourteen.

"Why do you want to join?" he was asked.

Still the boy didn't know, so again he was rejected.

He waited a bit longer, then returned and said he was sixteen.

"And why do you want to join the army?" he was asked.

This time he knew. "I want to overthrow the Nationalists," he replied briskly. "I want to strike down despots." He was accepted.

Chen Changfeng, another little red devil, had been even more stubborn. Told to come back when he was big enough to hold a rifle, he simply refused. He would not go back to a landlord who had stripped his house of every single possession when his father couldn't pay his debts. The landlord had even taken the boy's one quilt, and when the neighbors had begged for pity, he had tossed a broken saucepan back into the house. Young Chen broke into tears before the recruiting officer. "I will stay right here until you let me join," he cried. They gave in and taught him to be a bugler.

Now, several years later, Chen had been promoted. He was a bodyguard to Mao Zedong and wanted nothing more than to serve this tall, thin, mussed-up-looking man who had such big ideas for China and yet was so kind to young Chen. Take the day when Chen had discovered there was such a thing as a post office. Imagine, he'd told Mao—a place where a person could leave a letter and it would be delivered miraculously to another person far away! Mao had smiled and had sat right down to write a letter for Chen to send to his father. At the moment Mao, recovering from a bout of malaria, was being carried on a stretcher while Chen walked at his side, carrying Mao's personal possessions—two blankets, a cotton sheet, a worn overcoat, a broken umbrella, and a bundle of books.

Marching in front of Mao and Chen were other leaders— Zhu De, Zhou Enlai (who had come to Jiangxi at about the same time as Otto Braun and had taken over some of Mao's duties), and of course Otto Braun, who was directing the March.

But directing it where? Everyone was asking the same question as night after night passed and they seemed to be getting nowhere. Mile after mile. The distance between the soldiers and their homes kept widening and the new recruits wondered if they could ever find their way back. Never had they imagined such distance. Those in the vanguard or the advance units who were leading the way were especially troubled. One of their officers was Yang Chengwu, the young man who had found it so difficult to leave his father. They went to him. "Commissar, where are we going?" they asked. "When will this end?" But what could Yang say? He knew no more than they did about destinations.

But if the soldiers felt uneasy about the March, the porters, bent double by their heavy loads, groaned, grumbled, spat, and cursed. They had been hired at a dollar a day but they hadn't known how far they'd be going and they hadn't guessed how their poles would rub their shoulders raw, how their backs would strain, their legs knot, their feet stumble and give way. A tiny, four-foot-eleven woman, Liu Ying, had been given the job of trying to keep up the porters' spirits. If anyone could do it, the leaders said, she could. Such a fiery, persuasive woman, she had talked thousands of men in Jiangxi Province into joining the army. Now riding up and down on her small horse, she talked, she praised, she joked, she tried to will revolution into the souls of these suffering porters so their pain would not matter. But these men had moved beyond her reach. From time to time a group would simply drop their burdens, turn around, and head back home.

On October 21 Yang Chengwu's vanguard broke through the enemy's first line of barricades without trouble. On November 3 they broke through the second line. Scout Kong must have been right, they thought. The Nationalists weren't on the job. New recruits may have imagined that this was good news and that they could go home soon, but then suddenly in the middle of November they were ordered to march faster. Four hours of rest, four hours of marching night and day. Obviously the enemy was giving chase and tension crept among the ranks. The men didn't sleep as easily in their rest periods and when marching, they were always on the lookout.

By this time Yang Chengwu realized that they were moving toward the Xiang River, only 150 miles away, and were headed for northern Hunan and the Second Front Army. Yang urged his regiment ahead quickly and was surprised, as they all were, that still they met with no resistance. Not even from the last barricade of blockhouses. Once three Nationalist planes flew over and they thought that action had started, but Yang and the others threw themselves to the ground so quickly they weren't spotted. When they reached the Xiang River, all was quiet. They waded across the waist-deep water as if they were simply on an outing. Yang, however, was not fooled. He knew that there was trouble ahead, for Chiang Kai-shek would do anything to keep the various Red armies from uniting.

26

It was the central column that the Nationalists were after. Slowed down by fifty miles of groaning, baggage-laden porters, it did not reach the Xiang until twenty-four hours after the vanguard had crossed. By this time Chiang Kai-shek's troops were ready—300,000 men and several hundred planes. The trap was set. Hiding in forest on either side of the road, Nationalist soldiers fired at the Red soldiers as they passed. Overhead, Nationalist planes, swooping low, strafed the marching columns. Moreover, the blockhouses were fully manned now, and in order to pass them Red soldiers had to climb up the side of each one and throw a hand grenade through a porthole. It was a brutal scene. Although they pressed ahead, fighting every inch, whole companies of men—sometimes in the very act of crying *"Sha!"*—were cut down and silenced.

When the survivors finally reached the river, they found themselves in the dilemma that military men fear most. The army was cut in two. Part was on one side of the river; the rest was on the other side and the enemy was wedged around them. Yang Chengwu's vanguard regiment, thoroughly aroused, tried to help. Keeping up a steady fire on the enemy, they encouraged the central column to cross. Some did, but there was nothing orderly about what happened. It was shooting, shouting, wading, dying, drowning, scrambling across pontoons, horses rearing, whinnying, and a wholesale scuttling of equipment. Porters simply dumped their loads and disappeared. Cooks threw away pots and pans. Soldiers got rid of anything that they didn't consider essential. Many managed to get across the river safely, including the leaders and the headquarters units, but many lay where they'd been shot down.

Sometime during the confusion Yang Chengwu was wounded in the right knee. He was close enough to the enemy to hear their order to take him alive. Unable to walk, he expected to be captured at any moment. Nearby, another

Communist officer, critically wounded, had just committed suicide in order to avoid capture. But Yang's company commander ordered four soldiers to get Yang quickly out of danger as the rest of the company kept the enemy under fire. No stretchers were available, so they had to carry Yang in a stumbling, makeshift way and in the process two soldiers were killed. The other two survived and so did Yang.

By this time the rear guard had caught up to the rest of the army and could see the damage that had been done. Young Ding Ganru, who was seventeen but still called a little red devil because he was short and because he had joined at thirteen, felt as if he'd stumbled into the aftermath of a terrible storm. Hundreds of men were strewn across the ground. Shattered beyond repair, they looked as if they had simply been discarded, their faces frozen in whatever expression they had last worn. Not only had bodies been mowed down, but everything the army owned, it seemed, had been tossed and scattered about. Costumes for plays, cooking utensils, books, machines of all sorts. Paper money was floating down the surface of the river as if it were so much scrap.

Ding started to wade across the river but the current was so strong and he was so short that for a moment it seemed that he would be swept down the river along with the paper money.

Then a marshal riding across on horseback called to him. "Grab the tail of my horse, little devil; we'll get you across."

Ding grabbed and since the horse didn't seem to object, he held tight until they had reached the other side. Here, too, everything was a shambles. But at least Ding wasn't dead; he hadn't been captured; and he was across the river. When the army moved, he would be with it.

On December 3, after a week of fighting, the battle ended without a victory. Both sides simply quit. No one could say the Red troops had been defeated. They hadn't given up; they hadn't run away, but according to some estimates, they

28

had lost half their men. And they were mad. Ding Ganru thought the officers must be at fault. He'd fought in the April battle and seen the casualties then. And now even more! Scout Kong, who needed to blame someone, blamed the horses. They had balked as they were led over pontoons, and slowed down the crossing for everyone. Otto Braun picked on an officer. Every man in this officer's division had been killed, Braun pointed out, but *he* had managed to escape. He should be court-martialed. Mao Zedong didn't express his feelings, but there was no doubt that he agreed with another high-ranking officer who said that the only kind of battle Otto Braun knew how to fight was a battle on a map. Many, looking at Otto Braun with his big nose, must simply have cursed the day that he'd come to China.

No one talked of going home now. The Nationalists were behind them and the only way to leave the battle scene was up and over a mountain—Old Mountain, it was called. It was as steep as any mountain they had climbed, with a trail that was seldom more than two feet wide, and in their present condition the soldiers found this mountain the hardest they had met. During the fighting no one had time to feel tired, but now a terrible bone-weariness overcame the men. Some found themselves dropping off to sleep as they walked, their feet automatically taking steps while their minds closed down. The difficulty was not only that they had to get themselves up the mountain, they had to help others as well. So many had been injured, every stretcher was in use and every horse carried a wounded soldier. Those who had no means of transport put their arms around comrades and shuffled along. The thirty women, including Mao's wife, He Zizhen, who was expecting a baby soon, usually traveled in a group, but now they separated in order to give help where it was needed. Kang Keqing, who marched near her husband, loaded herself down with knapsacks and rifles of soldiers too exhausted to manage for themselves.

When it became dark, the traveling was more difficult and more dangerous. Not many, if any, had ever climbed Old Mountain before and those in the lead may not have been prepared for Thunder God Rock which stood at the top. A sheer rock face that reared up from the path at a ninety-degree angle, it had narrow steps for climbing but each step was waist-high. Still, they had no choice; it was either up those steps or off the cliff. At first the men tried to pull and push some of the horses up the steps but the horses could not make it. Many fell back to the path, their legs broken. It was just as impossible to carry stretchers up the steps and equally impossible in the dark to manage the wounded without stretchers. So the order went down the line: All should stay where they were. Sleep on the path and wait for daylight.

One soldier, wrapping himself in a blanket, knew that if he rolled over too far, he'd roll right off the cliff, so he tried not to fall into too deep a sleep. Later, when he remembered that night, he talked of the silence. It was so great, he said, he could hear it. "It was sometimes near, sometimes far away, sometimes loud, sometimes faint, and at other times like spring silkworms eating mulberry leaves."

Seen in the daylight the next morning, Thunder God Rock seemed no stranger than the rest of the scenery that the army had been passing through on the way to the Xiang River. In this part of the country the landscape all seemed freakish, as if a child had drawn it. Tall, monsterlike stones lined the riverbank; scallop-shaped hills made an embroiderylike boundary between the sky and the earth. It was a strange world that they were discovering; their experiences were strange. Yet even the most reluctant seemed to accept now that they were in for long, hard times together. Making a revolution, Mao Zedong said, was not a dinner party or writing an essay or painting a picture or doing embroidery. One had to expect violence and welcome hardship.

But they were certainly far from home. Coming down from Old Mountain, they thought that perhaps they had walked right out of China. When a squad leader spoke to a man, calling him "old cousin"—a familiar greeting—the man shook his head. He didn't understand. The squad leader tried three different dialects but still the man shook his head. Not only could the people not speak Chinese but they were too poor even to dress like Chinese. Some peasants had a few rags tied around them; a few, both men and women, had no clothes at all, yet they worked the land, pulling plows like field animals.

Mao Zedong explained that these were a minority people called the Miaos and warned his bodyguard, Chen Changfeng, that since they were a shy, suspicious people, nothing of theirs should be touched and nothing should even be bought from them. Chen knew the rules. Mao was very strict about the army paying for anything that came from peasants along the way. And if you took down a peasant's door to use as a bed, you must put it back the next day. Be honest, return what you borrow, be sanitary. But Chen could see there wasn't much that could be bought here and the doors to the houses weren't worth borrowing. Made of cornstalks and bamboo, they were too short and flimsy to be used as beds, and the houses themselves, hanging like baskets in the air, did not look sturdy enough to hold people who wore clothes. So the soldiers set up camp outside the village, cooked what rice they had, and fell asleep in a place where they were not scared to roll over.

Meanwhile the headquarters unit held a meeting. The question was: Where should the army go now? For the first time in two years Mao Zedong had been invited to participate in the discussion and he was quick to present his plan. They should abandon the idea of going to Hunan and joining the Second Front Army, he said. Chiang Kai-shek had too many troops ready to intercept them on that route. Instead they should march west, where the enemy was weaker. Later Mao was even more specific. They should capture the city of Zunyi on the other side of the Wu River and then hold a formal meeting to decide who their leaders should be. They could rest there, recruit, resupply themselves, and perhaps even establish Zunyi as their base. There was little argument. Zhou Enlai, who had already lost faith in Otto Braun, agreed with Mao's suggestions, and Zhu De was delighted that Mao was being heard again. Otto Braun had little to say.

Of course, Chen Changfeng had noticed that Mao was attending a lot of meetings these days. Mao had recovered from malaria, and although he had a big grayish-white horse which he had captured from the Nationalists in Jiangxi, usually he walked. Many nights, however, he worked so late that the next day he let his stretcher-bearers carry him a few hours so he could catch up on his sleep. Often at night Chen tried to stay up with Mao so, if asked, he could get Mao a cup of tea or a wet cloth to wipe his face; but when Mao saw Chen nodding off, he'd send him to bed. Chen obeyed reluctantly. Suppose Mao needed something? It was his job to see that Mao was well cared for. At night, for instance, when they stopped marching, Chen would look for the most sheltered spot and fix it up the way Mao liked—a board with a blanket over it for a bed, oilcloth overhead in case of rain, another board set up on some sort of base to serve as a desk. Chen was especially happy when a real house could be found, but this didn't happen often.

The army had left the Miao country far behind and were only thirty miles from the Wu River when they came into the busy market town of Houchang. It was the last day of December, cold, with snow on the ground, so everyone was hoping to find indoor shelter. Luckily some did. The house assigned to Mao was a happy-looking place with two snowmen guarding its front gate, probably the work of younger members of the wealthy family who had fled when they heard that the Communist Army was coming. (Wealthy people were not generally on the Communist side, nor Communists on their side.) Inside the gate was a large courtyard with rooms around it, but it was the interior of the house that Chen marveled at—carved furniture, pictures on the walls, kerosene lamps hanging from the ceilings. Chen was so pleased with the room he was preparing for Mao, he was determined to make this night special. On the hard bed where Mao would sleep, he and Mao's three other bodyguards piled straw to make it more comfortable. Once the straw was covered with a blanket, Chen may have tried lying down just to see how it would feel to sink into such softness, but he wouldn't have stayed long. The four bodyguards had an idea and they were eager to carry it out.

Mao was at a meeting, but since he had such fine quarters, might he not invite other leaders to his place afterward? And since this was New Year's Eve, wouldn't there be a celebration? Of course it was not the Lunar New Year that the Chinese celebrated, but still it was the official calendar New Year, always a time for a party. Back at Jiangxi, the army had enjoyed wonderful New Year's parties with games, competitions, and dramatic performances. One of the most popular games was "Pass the Handkerchief." Groups of officers and soldiers would sit together in a circle and as they clapped hands they would pass a handkerchief from one to another. Whoever was holding the handkerchief when the clapping stopped had to draw a question from a box in the center of the circle. If he could answer the question, he would be rewarded with peanuts; if he couldn't answer, he had to put on some kind of funny show to make the others laugh. Sometimes they played "Down with Chiang Kai-shek." They'd stand five sticks close together and try to knock them down with a pole thrown from a distance of about thirty feet. Those who could topple all five in one throw would be winners and of course there would be cheering, for every time there was a winner, Chiang Kai-shek would be the loser.

Tonight there wouldn't be games or much chance for merriment, but still, Chen said, they could prepare a feast and surprise Mao and his friends when they came back. So they hurried into town and were able to buy some of the foods that Mao liked best: beef chili, fried bean curd, and, best of all, sweet fermented rice prepared in such a way that it tasted like rice wine. They borrowed thirty stools in case the party turned out to be a large one.

At ten o'clock, when Mao came out of the meeting, Chen was waiting with a lantern to escort him and his friends home. But Mao was alone, tense and impatient. Of course Chen could not know that the leaders had found out that the enemy was moving toward the Wu River. Nor could he know that at the meeting Mao and Braun had openly disagreed on what the army should do. Braun said that they should stay where they were and fight there. Mao said they should cross the Wu River as fast as possible. The other leaders agreed with Mao and dispersed to give the army its orders.

Back at Mao's quarters, Chen pointed to the party all set up to celebrate the New Year. Anyone could see that guests were expected. They could still be invited, couldn't they?

Mao barely glanced at the table. The New Year? Mao acted as if the New Year was too frivolous even to think about. "We can't stay here," he said quickly. "We have to race across the Wu River and take Zunyi."

Chen couldn't keep the disappointment out of his voice. "But see," he said, "we have your favorite." He pointed to the sweet fermented rice.

Mao must have seen the stricken look on the faces of the bodyguards. He relented. At least they could eat the rice, he agreed, and sat down with his bodyguards to share this special treat.

34

Chen and his coworkers would have packed away the rest of the food to be eaten another time. It would not be wasted. Not like the bed. All that straw and no one to sleep in it!

Some soldiers setting out on that cold night may have been homesick for Jiangxi Province, but it would not have been wise for them to think about it. In November one city after another in Jiangxi had fallen to the Nationalists. Those soldiers who had remained had simply disappeared into the mountains or had taken up civilian life in the villages. People who had family members in the Red Army had pulled down the red banners on their doors. No, they would say when questioned, they'd had nothing to do with the Communists. Even so, thousands were killed. And on this New Year's Eve the landlords were back in control in Jiangxi.

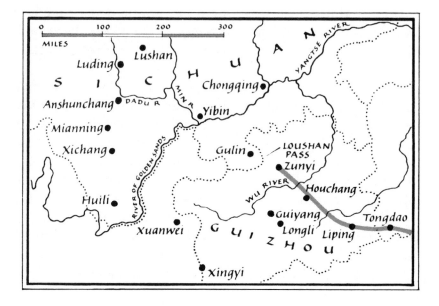

THREE

By the time Mao, his bodyguards, and the central column reached the Wu River, it was mid-morning of January 1, 1935. The vanguard, including Yang Chengwu (back on active duty), had arrived six hours before, but this was not a river just waiting tamely to be crossed. The Wu River was as fierce and angry-looking as if it were fighting on the enemy's side. Wide and wild at the bottom of two black cliffs, it tossed and foamed, waiting to strike out at all invaders. And on the slope of the opposite cliff, enemy units stood ready to back up the threats of the river.

Yang Chengwu could see that the vanguard could not possibly handle this river alone. The engineer corps was called and asked to figure out what could be done, and by the time the central column arrived, work had started. Men were rushing back to nearby villages to buy rope, to persuade peasants to sell the doors to their houses, to take whatever was needed from landlords, from those they called "bullies." Others were cutting down yellow bamboo trees which fortunately stood at hand. The plan was that the engineers would build rafts and join them together to make a long centipedelike floating bridge over which the entire army could march. But somehow a detachment of men had to be placed first on the other side of the river so that it could keep those enemy posts under fire while the bridge was being built.

Swimmers would cross first, laying a rope in the water to help others cross. But as it turned out, not many men could swim. Most had been brought up in the interior of China with no experience in the water; still, in the end eighteen swimmers were rounded up. Eight were told to swim with one arm while releasing the rope with the other. Once across, they would be joined by raftloads of men and fighting equipment. Not until a whole platoon had landed, however, would they begin shooting.

The river was green, icy cold, and 250 feet wide, but the swimmers were halfway across when the rope they were holding was severed by enemy shells. One of the eight swimmers was wounded. So there was nothing to do but turn around and swim back. The first raft, following close behind, was also unlucky. In the middle of the river it was hit by enemy fire and overturned. All came back safely, however, except for the wounded man, who froze and drowned on the way.

Now they abandoned the idea of swimmers and decided that the rafts would cross at night when they wouldn't be seen. Four rafts were made ready but the third and fourth were ordered not to leave until after the second raft had signaled with a flashlight that it had landed safely. For the most part, men who could swim were chosen to man the rafts in case of accidents, and since Mao Zedong prided himself on being a strong swimmer, he went in command of the second raft. Young Chen Changfeng would probably not have seen Mao leave, because only those with business on the riverbank would have been allowed there. If Chen had known, he would have worried.

Certainly the men on the riverbank worried as they waited for that light to flash. One hour went by. Two hours. Still there was no signal and since no one swam ashore, they had to believe that Mao's raft had been lost. What was more, those on the first raft returned by foot to the launching site. They had been swept downriver by the current and forced to land on their own side. So after a day and a night the Red Army was still on the wrong side of the river.

Well, then, they would try again in the daylight. They would be seen but at least they would be able to see where they were going. At nine o'clock the next morning three more rafts set out and this time luck was with the rafters. Although the enemy did fire on them, no one was hurt and, even luckier, the enemy itself was suddenly attacked. That second raft which everyone thought had been lost had actually landed under the rocks where the enemy was posted. Mao and the others had not dared use a flashlight for fear they would be discovered, and although they had tried lighting matches, the flames had been too tiny to be seen. Now they came out of hiding and distracted the enemy with their fire while the three rafts pulled safely to shore.

Meanwhile the bridge builders were having trouble. It was raining, the hands of the workers were numb with cold, enemy shells kept dropping around them, wounding some, killing others. Besides, the bridge itself was not working. They had made a hundred rafts but when they tied the first few sections together and put them in the water, they bounced about like toys. Of course as more sections were added, they would only bounce more. They would have to anchor the bridge or it would be swept away long before it reached the other side.

Shi Changjie, a tall, sturdy young man who had been a boatman before joining the army, was put in charge of anchoring the bridge. At first rocks were used but the ones the men could find were all too smooth to grip the river bottom and too light to hold. Then someone thought of baskets. Fortunately there was enough bamboo, so people were put to work all along the riverbank, cutting the bamboo into strips, weaving the strips into large baskets, driving three sharp logs through the middle of each basket to dig into the river bottom. Finally they filled the baskets with stones and attached a cable to each basket. Shi Changjie put one of the baskets on a raft, poled his way to a bridge section, attached the cable to the bridge, and dropped the basket. It worked!

Encouraged, everyone worked faster but no one with more enthusiasm than Shi Changjie. Proud to put his skill as a boatman to such important use, he poled back and forth, attaching new sections to the lengthening bridge and dropping anchors. The bridge was 150 feet long with only 100 feet more to go, when the pole Shi Changjie was using was hit by a bullet and shattered. Since he had extra poles, he picked up a new one and continued on his way, but this too was hit and broken. Again he replaced it and again it was hit, but the poles were not the real target of the enemy. Shi Changjie was the target and the next bullet found its mark and struck him. The bridge builders saw Shi go down and they also saw that his raft was rushing out of control, heading directly for the center of the completed part of the bridge. If it hit, the bridge would be destroyed.

Shouting and scrambling, the men rushed to avert the collision, but Shi, wounded as he was, recognized the danger and jumped into the water, hoping that he could lessen the impact. As it turned out, there was no impact. The bridge builders were on time to save the bridge, but there was no way to save Shi Changjie. When they pulled him out of the water, he was dead. He was not the first victim of the Wu River but his death affected the army as none other had. They finished building the bridge in a burst of defiance, angry at both the river and the enemy. And when, in the early hours of January 3, the army crossed the completed bridge, they marched four abreast, bugles blowing as if they had won a victory, as indeed they had. The enemy recognized it and retreated.

Many men had not slept or eaten a real meal for thirty-six hours, so everyone was looking forward to Zunyi, where they were promised a rest and where, it was rumored, they might even stay. But they would have to capture the city first. A regiment of 1,000 men from the vanguard was sent ahead to do the job although they were warned that inside the walls of the city 3,000 soldiers would be ready to oppose them. What they didn't know was that first they would have to capture an enemy outpost stationed ten miles from the city. At four o'clock on the morning of January 4, while they were sleeping in a village still thirty miles from Zunyi, a scout reported the presence of that outpost. Everyone was ordered to report immediately to the regimental commander for orders.

It was pouring rain. Dripping and shivering, the men stood before their commander as he told them to proceed full speed ahead so that they could surprise the outpost. When they had taken it, they were to continue to Zunyi. The men should steel themselves, the commander shouted, to meet tough resistance. "Be prepared to slice rocks," he cried, "even if the enemy turns out to be as soft as bean curds." (When the Red soldiers were doing well, they often referred to the Nationalists as "bean-curd troops.")

The men responded with shouts and raised fists and set off at a brisk pace in a heavy rain that fooled the enemy into a false sense of security. Who would go out in such weather?

they asked. Caught off guard, they did indeed become bean-curd troops, terrified of their captors.

A captain in the Red Army regiment took twelve prisoners aside.

"Why did you enlist?" he asked.

They were starving, they replied. What else could they do?

"Do you know why we are fighting?" the captain asked.

They knew only what their officers told them, they said. According to their officers, the Communists were horrible red-nosed, blue-eyed monsters who loved to kill and gouge out the eyeballs of their captives. Although they could see that the Communists were neither red-nosed nor blue-eyed, they may still have worried about their eyeballs. Still, when each of these twelve was given three silver dollars and in-vited to join the Red Army, each accepted. Their first assign-ment, the captain said, was to lend the Red soldiers their Nationalist uniforms, lead them to Zunyi, and then pretend that the Reds were part of their own army. Captives who spoke in the local dialect would tell the sentries to open the gates, for the trick wouldn't work if a Jiangxi man spoke. He'd be suspected immediately.

It was shortly after midnight and still raining when the army reached the city gates.

"Who goes there?" a sentry called from the gate tower.

One of the captured men replied as he'd been coached. "Friends," he cried. "Your own men. The Reds are after us. Hurry! Open up!"

Flashlights from the tower played upon the men below and when the sentries saw the Nationalist caps, they un-bolted the gates.

"Have the Reds really crossed the Wu?" a sentry asked.

The Communist regiment rushing through the gates as-sured the sentry that yes, the Reds had really crossed the Wu. And now they were taking Zunyi. Thirty regimental bu-glers blew the call to charge which awakened the city. Nationalist soldiers poured out of bed and into a battle which continued for several days. Still, the residents of Zunyi must have decided early that the Reds were going to win. The wealthy ones, those who might suffer at the hands of the Communist Army, made a hasty retreat before the battle was over. Some of the military men too. At the same time those Zunyi people who had been working underground for the Communist cause came into the open to help their comrades.

By January 8 the opposition was over. The Communist troops occupied the city of Zunyi and the entire population turned out to celebrate and to prepare for the arrival of the leaders and the rest of the army. The next day there was a grand entry. Almost as if the new leadership had already been decided, Mao led the way on horseback through the city gates and into the cheering crowds, into a city festooned with red banners and exploding with firecrackers. The Communist soldiers had been successful before, but when had they been given such a welcome?

As soon as the festivities were over, orderlies and bodyguards were put to work preparing the quarters that the leaders would use. A large, square, charcoal-colored house with white columns, formerly owned by a local warlord, was chosen as the headquarters and residence for Zhou Enlai and his wife, for Zhu De and Kang Keqing, and for a number of those in top positions. Mao and two other leaders occupied a similar house, but since both houses had been abandoned in a hurry, the floors were littered and needed a thorough cleaning.

It was while Zhou Enlai's bodyguard, Wei Guolu, was sweeping out Zhou's room that he noticed something gold glittering on the floor. Wei, formerly a cowherd in a poor family, had never seen a ring but he knew what it was. He also knew that real gold when put under a flame would not tarnish or melt, so he tested it. It was real gold and, slipping it on a finger, he decided he liked the idea of wearing a ring. He had been trained by the army not to take anything that didn't belong to him, but this didn't seem like taking. It was only finding and keeping, so he was surprised the next morning when Zhou spoke to him.

"Do you understand the army rules?" he asked.

Well, of course Wei understood them. The Three Main Rules of Discipline and the Eight Points of Attention. Hadn't he recited them every day? Hadn't he sung them with the army as they marched, even as they marched into Zunyi?

"Then what is that thing on your finger?" Zhou asked. "When we say everything taken from local tyrants should be turned in, we mean everything."

It was the Third Rule. "Turn in everything you capture." Wei hadn't thought that picking something out of the dust was capturing, but if he had actually captured something from a tyrant, it made him feel important. So he apologized and went quickly to his political instructor to turn in the ring.

In Mao's house Chen Changfeng was having a fine time serving real meals, not just marching rations. Back in Jiangxi Chen had given Mao his favorite breakfast every morning: American oatmeal with condensed milk and two eggs beaten in it, but even if he'd been able to find oatmeal on the March, Mao wouldn't have eaten it. He ate only what the soldiers ate—no special treats. In Zunyi, however, everyone could eat well. There may not have been oatmeal available but Chen discovered a restaurant that made another of Mao's favorite dishes: Moon and Four Stars—layers of lamb, fish, chicken, vegetables, and taro root steamed into a kind of giant sandwich without bread. It cost only a dollar so Chen (as well as many other soldiers) became a regular customer.

Everyone in the city, it seemed, was busy. New straw sandals had to be made for the army, new padded jackets for the cold weather, new soldiers recruited for the Communists' dwindling forces. Four thousand Zunyi men enlisted as a result of the whirlwind campaign that little Liu Ying and her recruiters conducted.

But no one had to recruit seventeen-year-old Li Xiauxia; she would have been one of the first to volunteer for the army. Criticized for being a tomboy as a young girl, she was now an ardent Communist who, more than anything, wanted to change the life that women led in China. When as a student representative she was asked to address a mass rally for 10,000, she recognized that here was her first chance to speak out for women.

Why should women be second-class citizens? she cried. They weren't allowed to argue with men; they weren't allowed to speak to boys, even boy cousins; and wherever a girl went, she had to be accompanied by an older person. Why? Why couldn't they go where they wanted alone? Looking at her audience, she could see many women tottering on tiny misshapen clumps of feet. When they had still been little girls, their feet had been bound, their toes mashed painfully under each other so they'd grow up with what were called "lily feet." Many men wouldn't marry women unless they had lily feet. But why should women submit to such inhuman treatment? Why should they be constantly humiliated? She remembered her sister who had been tortured by her husband and died a year after her arranged marriage, and she begged these Chinese standing before her to help free women. Let them be independent. Let them be partners in building a new China.

When Li Xiauxia had finished, she was excited. She wanted to find new audiences and go on talking like this. Perhaps when she marched with the Red Army, she thought, she would have that chance.

And it seemed that the army would go on marching. Perhaps even before they reached Zunyi, the leaders had realized that Zunyi would not make a good base after all.

Bounded by three rivers, it could easily be encircled and the army would be trapped. Furthermore, they learned that Nationalist troops were in the south, not too far away. So the Communists decided to go north, cross the Yangtse River, and try to join Zhang Guotao and his Fourth Front Army in Sichuan Province. They didn't know just where the Fourth Front was, but they hoped to find it near the southern border.

Meanwhile there was the matter of leadership to be decided. Who was to be in charge? For three nights beginning on January 15 the leaders gathered at seven o'clock in that large, square headquarters building to plan for the future. As far as is known, there was no official vote taken. Mao simply took over the meeting, criticizing the tactics that had been so disastrous and offering his own ideas. Zhou Enlai and Zhu De were put jointly in charge of military operations; Otto Braun was ousted from power and the man in top command was Mao Zedong. Chairman Mao, he would be called.

The army of course rejoiced that Mao was back in charge, but not all the army knew it right away. Yang Chengwu, for instance, was already headed north with his vanguard units to open a way to the Yangtse River. They'd been sent out of Zunyi, Yang complained, before they'd even had a chance to warm their bottoms. And certainly without a chance to taste Zunyi's famous Moon and Four Stars or any of its cakes. Even the regiment commander felt a little cross and when they passed a village shop with eggcakes in the window, he couldn't help remarking on how good they looked. Eggcakes were a great delicacy. Riding a mule nearby, his bodyguard overheard the remark and thought how easily he could please his commander. So he turned his mule around and raced back for the eggcakes. When he returned, he handed a large package to the commander, announcing with pride that here were some eggcakes.

The commander opened the package. "Eggcakes!" he exclaimed. "Why, you country bumpkin! These are just common ricecakes."

The bodyguard didn't see much difference. "This is the kind of eggcakes we had in Jiangxi," he said. After all, in Jiangxi food was food; cakes were cakes; they'd had few delicacies and little variety. In the lean days at their home base they had lived on nothing but squash and made a joke of it. "Down with capitalism," they had cried, "and eat squash!" But whatever kind of cakes these were, they were better than squash and better than no cakes at all.

Obviously there were not enough cakes to go around and the spirits of the men remained low until they heard that they were to spend the night at a fancy resort town. Usually the town was occupied by wealthy Nationalists but they had abandoned it because of the fighting. So there would be empty houses to sleep in. Western-style houses, they were told, lighted by electricity. Many of the men had never seen electricity and it seemed like magic to think of glass bulbs lighting up without anyone even applying a match.

They arrived at four o'clock in the afternoon. Members of the platoon that Yang Chengwu was with entered the house assigned to them, and yes, there were bulbs but they had no light in them. Nor could they make light, they were told. The generator at the power plant had run out of coal so it was not working.

Some of the men went to the power plant. Where was the coal? they asked.

It was on the other side of the mountain, they were told, but the truck that was used to haul it had been taken by the Nationalists when they left.

Well, these men had no intention of missing a chance to see electricity. Forming themselves into teams, using whatever containers they could find, they went to the other side of the mountain and carried the coal back themselves.

But before the generator could be started, orders came

that the men had to move on immediately. Word had been received that the enemy was gathering ahead; they could not stop overnight as planned.

Wearily the men dragged themselves into marching formation, too accustomed to disappointment to do more than mutter among themselves. Ahead of them ridge after ridge of hills rose like an obstacle course to be surmounted. Why was it, they asked themselves, that they not only had to fight the enemy but had constantly to fight the land as well?

It was long past dark as they wound up to the summit of the first hill. Then, glancing back at the town they had just left, they broke into a cheer. The place was sparkling with lights. Electric lights! The generator was back at work and every light in town, it seemed, had been turned on as a signal of greeting to them, a signal of encouragement, a signal of triumph. Even those who were familiar with electricity took heart as they looked at that bright patch in the black night.

War was changing the men in the army. Often small triumphs seemed for the moment as important as big triumphs. Indeed, time itself had changed with no divisions left in it. What was the difference now between night and day? Between one week and another? And what was the difference between one's own self and one's comrades? Life had become such a joint affair, they felt they were going through it in a solid body. Even years later veterans of the Long March would invariably say "we" rather than "I" when they talked of those old days.

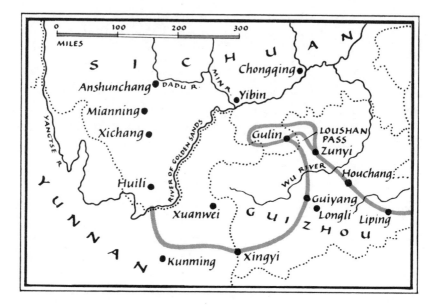

FOUR Before Otto Braun had taken over, surprise had been the secret weapon of the Communist Army, and surprise was again what it was counting on as it rushed toward the Yangtse River. This time, however, it was the Communist Army that was taken by surprise. The Nationalists, who had not been able to stop the Red troops at the Xiang River or at the Wu, were determined to keep them from crossing the Yangtse. And they did. Yang Chengwu and his vanguard units were stopped cold. Twenty miles away Mao's own forces found themselves suddenly face to face with 10,000 crack Sichuan troops commanded by a famous general nicknamed Panda. Although the Red soldiers fought fiercely, they were caught in a battle so serious that after one night and one day, Mao ordered them to retreat and move west. China was a big country,

48

Mao said; the Yangtse was a long river. They'd cross it at another point, but hardly had they started when they discovered that the enemy was also moving west.

Well, then, they'd go back to Zunyi and start over. Only this time they would take such a roundabout route, the enemy would never guess where they were. Unfortunately, however, before they could enter Zunyi, they'd have to fight another battle. The city had been reoccupied by the enemy almost as soon as they had left so there was nothing to do but capture it again. Moreover, before they even reached Zunyi, they would have to go through Loushan Pass, a narrow cleft in the mountains where, it was said, a few men in control could keep a whole army at bay. So although the Communist troops marched one way, changed direction, marched another, all the time they headed for Zunyi and Loushan Pass, and all the time they hurried.

On the way, Chinese New Year came and went as if it had been any other day in the year. This was the beginning of the Year of the Pig, but there was neither time nor opportunity to celebrate. And there was no point thinking about family and feasts. Most soldiers didn't know if they still had families and didn't want to think about feasts. Most had eaten nothing for two days.

On the way, He Zizhen, Mao's wife, gave birth to the baby she'd been expecting. There was no time to find shelter, to rest, to become acquainted with her baby except to notice that it was a boy. There was no time to let Mao know about the baby. No time to give the baby a name. Like all women who gave birth on the March, she knew it was impossible to keep the baby with her. So the baby was wrapped in a piece of black cloth and given, along with some silver dollars, to a peasant family who agreed to raise him. He Zizhen wouldn't have complained. If she had, Liu Ying would have asked her what she asked all young mothers who resisted giving up their babies. "Which do you love more, your child or the

49

Revolution?" It was sad, Liu Ying admitted, but that's the way it was. And no woman who had gone this far on the March would have renounced the Revolution.

On February 24, as the army came within striking distance of Loushan Pass, an argument developed between two generals. One said that since they were all tired and since there was no sign of the enemy at the pass, they could slow down and take it easy. The other general insisted that they should continue just as fast as they possibly could. The leaders decided on speed and, as it turned out, that was wise.

On the morning of February 26 the Red Army heard that the enemy troops were just eleven miles from Loushan Pass and advancing rapidly. At that moment the Reds were also eleven miles from the pass on the opposite side, so it was a race to see who could move faster. Tired as they were, the Red troops were used to pushing themselves hard. They arrived at Loushan at three in the afternoon, not more than five minutes ahead of the enemy, just two or three hundred yards away. This gave the Reds control of the pass, and although fighting continued all the way to Zunyi, they fought as if nothing could or would stop them. In the end 3,000 Nationalists were captured, along with 1,000 rifles and 100,000 rounds of ammunition. It was one of the Communist Army's biggest victories.

But of course the Communist troops suffered losses too. Often it was not the number who were wounded and killed that was felt as keenly as the specific men who were lost. Yang Chengwu, for instance, lost one of his best friends at the pass. Yang was walking with the communications platoon, as he often did just because this platoon was such a fun-loving, lively group, forever singing, laughing, practicing entertainment acts to perform for the army during rest periods. The platoon leader, eighteen-year-old Little Xie, who was Yang's special friend, was particularly peppy and full of ideas for putting on skits. He would improvise songs

as he marched along, singing as the platoon clapped in time to his music. Perhaps because it was so foggy as they marched toward the pass, the platoon found their jokes funnier than usual, for their laughter, exploding here and there in the fog, sounded unattached to living people, as if it were coming from the clouds.

Yang and Little Xie, walking side by side, had not been able to see each other for much of the time, but as the fog cleared, they first heard and then saw planes approaching.

"Planes!" Little Xie shouted. "Fall down! Fall down!" He pushed Yang into a gully and dropped down beside him. Other members of the platoon fell to the ground wherever they were.

Three planes dived toward the marching men, dropped bombs, then, shrieking into the sky, roared off.

Yang Chengwu stood up but Little Xie did not move. He was lying on his back, his chest covered with blood. Other platoon members gathered around Little Xie. "You can't die!" they cried. "Platoon leader! Don't die! Don't die!" But Little Xie did die and sixteen other platoon members as well. As Yang held Little Xie in his arms, he looked at the sky and at the rolling mountains. All looked so permanent. How could it be that life could just stop? As if it were no more than a match with its flame puffed out.

Scout Kong was another victim of a bombing although he survived. One of four scouts who were taking turns wearing the one heavy jacket allotted them, he was just south of Loushan Pass when bomb fragments tore into his hip. Like all the wounded, he was carried into a Catholic church at Zunyi which the Communists had turned into a temporary hospital. The building was filled with casualties but Scout Kong was the noisy one. Delirious, running a high fever, he shouted as if he were still in battle. *"Sha!"* he yelled. All night he continued his imaginary charge against the enemy. *"Sha! Sha!"* No matter how often the other patients begged him to quiet down, Scout Kong never stopped.

The army stayed in Zunyi only a couple of days, but when they left, Scout Kong was with them on a stretcher. His wound was not healing, however, and after two weeks it was clear that he was too sick to continue. Normally a man of his rank would have been given a few dollars and left with peasants, but because Scout Kong was so famous for his bravery, he was given special attention. Put in the home of a sympathetic landlord who swore to be true to the Red Army, Scout Kong was left in the care of a doctor and an orderly, given three hundred dollars and a large supply of medicine. Of course his days of scouting and crying "Sha!" were over, and although he had to stay in bed for a year and a half, he did recover. He began to get better, he said later, as soon as all the hair on his head was shaved off. In any case, he was able eventually to lead a normal life.

Li Xiauxia, the young girl who had spoken at the Zunyi rally, was also one who started on the Long March but was not allowed to continue to the end. When the army entered Zunyi for the second time, Li found her house in shambles and all her family killed. This made her more determined than ever to fight with the Red Army, but after being on the road for a short time, she was told to go back to Zunyi. The Nationalists would occupy it again and she would do more for the Revolution if she went underground and fought as a guerrilla in the territory she knew best. She didn't want to return. She longed to stay with the army, to meet hardships with them, to share their revolutionary spirit. But Mao himself told Li she must go back and she did. She became a deputy leader of the guerrilla forces, faced great trials, and had narrow escapes. As an old woman looking back on those days, she smiled. She had a pistol and used it well, she said. Still, she would have liked to have stayed with the army on its Long March.

As the soldiers left Zunyi, they were in high spirits. This time they had not simply escaped defeat, they had actually scored a victory. They had new confidence and they were spreading their revolution as they traveled. In every village they passed through, propaganda teams prepared the way for the army's entrance—writing slogans on the walls, putting up posters, explaining the principles of their revolution. They put on shows and sang together. Zhu De made up one of their songs:

> *You are poor, I am poor,*
> *Of ten men, nine are poor.*
> *If the nine men unite,*
> *How can the tiger landlords fight?*

As the army whipped up enthusiasm in the countryside, that enthusiasm in turn stirred the army with a renewed sense of purpose and a deeper sense of brotherhood. The soldiers had no clear picture of what life would be like after the Revolution, but they knew it would be better.

Meanwhile they were learning as they marched. In a new China, it was agreed, everyone should be able to read. So why wait? Each soldier wore a white cloth on his back with a character (or word) written on it so the soldier behind could learn as he marched. Each day the character was changed. The longer they marched, the more words the soldiers knew, and soon they were able to read the rules and slogans they had memorized, which they chanted in order to keep them fresh in mind. After all, they were expected not only to preach revolution but to remember the rules so well that they would practice them.

Of course they became tired as they marched. Later the soldiers would say that they were always sleepy during the Long March and almost always hungry, but they understood that their success depended upon speed and surprise. And now they were out to fool the Nationalists. Going one way, doubling back, crossing rivers, recrossing them, the soldiers themselves were often frustrated because they didn't seem to be getting anywhere, yet they were always rushing.

To the peasants, however, the Red Army seemed to be

everywhere at once. How did they do it? They must have magic instruments, they decided. Extra legs to help them march so fast; magic devices to help them hear sounds from a great distance; and some kind of river-crossing magic, for as everyone could see, they had no boats.

But if the peasants were impressed, the enemy was confused. Once Chiang Kai-shek thought the Red Army was moving back to Jiangxi; indeed, he didn't know where the army was going. Sometimes the enemy was so mixed up, they'd fly over Red troops, thinking they were their own men. Three Nationalist trucks once drove right up to a column of Red soldiers, not realizing who they were until they were suddenly surrounded and their tires blown out. The trucks were loaded with hams, tea, and medical supplies, which of course the Red soldiers were delighted to have. They even found a local map, which they had needed. How nice of the enemy, they laughed, to give them just what they wanted! After this they often made a joke when they saw the Nationalists coming. "Here come our supplies!" they'd cry.

But the leaders knew where they were going. Still determined to cross the Yangtse, they were headed for an unlikely part of the river, far to the south and west of the point they had originally hoped to cross. This part of the river isn't even called the Yangtse but is known as the River of Golden Sands, a treacherous waterway which runs swiftly between towering gorges. There were a few ferry crossings in the southern loop of the river but these were in the hands of the Nationalists, who could not imagine that a whole army would ever try to cross there. Although the river was narrow, it was far too deep for wading and far too dangerous for swimming. Boats were needed but the Nationalists had all the boats. Besides, at the moment the Nationalists believed that the Red Army had another objective in mind. They were marching directly for Kunming, the capital of the province of Yunnan, and to protect the city Chiang Kai-shek recalled three of his regiments stationed on the River of Golden Sands.

This was exactly what Mao Zedong wanted Chiang to do. His plan to deceive the enemy was working, for those Red soldiers marching toward Kunming were only part of the army (10,000 men including Yang Chengwu). And they were just putting on a show to scare the Nationalists. On April 29 they climbed a hill eight miles from Kunming so everyone in the city could take a good look at them. Then they disappeared.

Meanwhile Mao and the rest of the army were headed for the River of Golden Sands but the question was: Would they be able to cross it? Could they get across before Chiang Kaishek realized what was going on and caught up with them? Already on Chiang's orders, the boats (at least all they knew of) had been tied on the north side of the river, out of the Communists' reach. Now he was sending his men in pursuit of those troops that appeared at Kunming but were hurrying toward the river.

But he didn't count on how fast the Red soldiers could move. The troops that Yang Chengwu was with had been told that if they did not reach the crossing by May 7, the army might have to go on without them. So these troops didn't just march; they kept up a running jog. At one stretch they covered a hundred miles in forty-eight hours, although some men dropped out, unable to keep up the pace. In the final two days they covered fifty to sixty particularly rough miles but they made the deadline. It is not surprising that the enemy didn't catch them.

By this time the Red soldiers were across the river. They had found a couple of boats, and by dressing up in captured Nationalist uniforms they had been able to subdue the sentries and customs officers on the other side of the river. Altogether they seized seven boats and thirty-six boatmen. The large boats carried sixty men and the smaller ones carried twenty. The horses, who refused to climb in the boats, were held by their halters and swam alongside. It took only three minutes to make the crossing, but even so, it was nine days and nine nights before the soldiers, including the Kunming men, were safely across. Enemy planes flew over but the river gap was too narrow for them to be able to bomb it. Two days later, after the Red soldiers had destroyed the boats and were still catching their breath on the far side of the river, the enemy arrived.

"Come on over!" the Reds called cheerily. "The swimming is fine!"

Chen Changfeng, Mao's bodyguard, had never worried about whether the army would be able to cross the River of Golden Sands. He never worried about what the army would do next. His responsibility was Mao Zedong himself and that was enough to keep him busy. Crossing the river with Mao in one of the first boatloads on May 1, Chen was already concerned about what kind of quarters he could establish for Mao on the other side. Even in the dark he could tell he would have trouble. A sheer rocky cliff rose up from a flinty beach which held out little hope for comfort or cover. Yet when he landed and began to explore, Chen found that there were ledges in the cliff with a steep path leading from one to another. As Mao went to confer with other leaders, Chen climbed the path and found on the second ledge a series of eleven caves. Actually they were little more than holes dug by rivermen into a sandy stretch in the cliff, yet they had obviously been used as shelter in the past and were the best quarters the landscape had to offer. So Chen took one cave for Mao, and the bodyguards of other commanders took the rest.

But how was Chen to fix up the cave? There was no wood available that could be turned into a desk for Mao to use. No door to serve as a bed. So he spread out the oilcloth on the sandy floor, covered it with a blanket, and although he knew

58

Mao would want to work, he didn't see what he could do about a desk. Mao liked to have his maps pinned on a wall beside his work table, but these walls were so sandy they crumbled when Chen tried to hang the maps up. Chen shrugged. Well, at least he could boil some water and have that ready for Mao when he came in.

He was still tending to the water when Mao returned and called for him.

"Everything ready?" Mao asked.

"I've done all that I can," Chen replied, pointing to the makeshift bed.

"What about a place to work?" Mao asked.

"I couldn't find anything to use as a desk," Chen explained, and he offered to bring Mao some boiled water. But Mao showed no interest in water.

"Don't you know yet," he asked, "that work is the all-important thing? Now find me a board or something to use as a desk."

Chen should have known, he told himself. Hadn't he watched Mao night after night working with telegrams and documents spread out on his desk? Hadn't he seen him busy with the field telephone, always trying to figure out the next step?

Chen went to look again. Of course he had to find something. Mao was not a person who took no for an answer. Wasn't he always telling the story of the man who refused to believe he couldn't move a mountain? And the man did move it, a spoonful at a time. This time Chen was determined, and as he scoured the area, he finally came across a board that looked as if it had once served as a door to a cave.

Together he and Mao set up the board and spread out maps and papers on it. For the next three days and nights Mao never left his desk. Chen had no idea what Mao was planning, and it was not Chen's business. But never again would he fail to supply Mao with a desk.

Actually, as Mao was studying his maps, he was trying to figure out how the First Front Army could join forces with Zhang Guotao and the Fourth Army. They were in Sichuan Province now, where Zhang was supposed to be, and although he didn't know just where Zhang was, he guessed that his men would have to march north. They would have to cross the Dadu River, probably at a point some 500 or more miles away.

His soldiers would all have heard of the Dadu, no matter where they had come from. Certainly they would all have heard the story of the Dadu that had been told and retold throughout China, with so many scary endings added over the years that many Chinese had become superstitious about the Dadu. It was here, a hundred years before, so the story went, that 40,000 warriors of another famous rebellion had been killed and their bodies thrown in the river. Ever since, their spirits were said to haunt the place and moan on dark nights.

Mao paid no attention to such superstitions but he did know that of all the rivers they had crossed, the Dadu might be the hardest. Moreover, Nationalist troops would certainly try to prevent them from crossing.

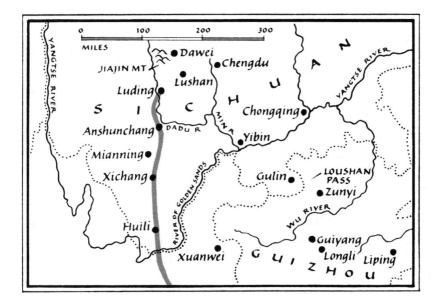

FIVE 卍卐 The Communist Army, which had started out in the autumn of 1934, had marched through winter and into spring. Certainly it was pleasant to leave the cold behind and to see the Sichuan countryside suddenly ablaze with flowers. Azaleas plunging down the hillsides. Irises, oleanders, roses scattering color as if color were meant for spending. Zhu De, who had always loved flowers, would have appreciated the scenery more than most of the men. The first thing he remembered in his childhood, he said, was the sight of flowers. He'd marveled at them then and he marveled at them now. But to most, the land, beautiful as it might be, had become something to be conquered, miles that had to be covered, footstep by footstep, territory that was judged by the difficulties it presented.

It was a help now, however, for the soldiers to know that

they had at least a temporary destination. Looking at the map, Mao had picked the city of Huili, where, if all went well, he hoped the army could take a rest and the leaders could hold a meeting. It had been four months since they had met at Zunyi, and with the army down to about 20,000 men from 86,000, there should be a reorganization. Besides, Mao knew that a few of the generals were complaining—in particular Lin Biao, commander of the First Army, the vanguard group in which Yang Chengwu served. It was Lin Biao's army that always had to make the fast marches and it was Lin Biao who had wanted to take it easy on the way to Loushan Pass but had been overruled. So if differences existed, Mao decided, they should be aired.

There were many towns in Sichuan where the people, already sympathetic to Communism, cheered the soldiers on their arrival, brought them baskets of fruit, set off firecrackers. But Huili was not such a place. There the Nationalists were in control and the city had not just one wall around it but a moat and two walls, an inner one and an outer one. The Red soldiers managed to get through two of the gates in the first wall. But then they were stopped. First by fires.

The fires were set in the area between the two walls which held many small huts. Still, fires could be fought and eventually the Reds overcame them and prepared to attack the second wall. They set up bamboo scaling ladders against the wall but the people in Huili were ready for them. As the men began to climb the ladders, the townspeople climbed ladders on their side of the wall. They carried huge vats of scalding porridge—a thin mixture that poured readily. They dumped it, vat by vat, on the heads of the invading soldiers.

Guns were one thing, fire another, but how could an army fight hot porridge? That was too much. The Communist troops retreated and the leaders held their meeting in an abandoned blacksmith's shop outside the walls.

Lin Biao listed his complaints. Mao was pushing the army too hard, he said. The soldiers were all exhausted. Moreover, Mao always took the long route, wherever he was going. Why didn't he ever take a short cut? It was as if the army were following the outside of a circle when they might be taking a direct course through the center. And where were they going? It was May and still they had not joined up with either of the other armies, nor had they established a base of their own. Finally, Lin Biao proposed that Mao step down as commander of field operations and manage only political policy.

Not for one minute did Mao take seriously the suggestion of stepping down. It was as if he could physically feel the future of China lying in his own hands and in his own hands only. All his life he held tight to his power. He brushed aside Lin Biao's proposal but he did explain why the army took a curving rather than a straight route. The army was in the pocket of the enemy, he said. They had to move back and forth; they had to use surprises; they had to follow the curve of a bowl rather than cut across the middle. The leaders accepted Mao's argument; they accepted Mao and agreed to his plan to cross the Dadu River. When they were ready to move on, the army was organized into more efficient units with the number of divisions reduced. And Liu Ying took on the job of secretary to the Central Committee. She had never done work like this before but she soon learned how to take minutes and to keep records. Nothing was ever too hard for Liu Ying.

As the army moved toward the Dadu, everyone understood that again they were racing the Nationalists to a river crossing, but this time there was an undercurrent of dread. Maybe the stories about the Dadu were only superstition; still, it was a fact that an army of rebel soldiers had met their fate there or, if not there, not far away. How could they be sure that their spirits didn't still haunt the place, pulling living people into the river and turning them into "water devils"? Chiang Kai-shek was boasting that at the Dadu the Red Army, like that other rebel army, would be finished off. Could the past rise up, the soldiers asked, and repeat itself?

Mao reassured them. No, he said. "The past does not return. We are revolutionaries. History has changed; we have changed."

This may have been comforting, but still an uneasy feeling hung over the army entering unknown territory where strange forces might be at work.

Strange people too. Before they reached the Dadu, the Communist troops had to pass through the land of another minority people, the Yis, who were said to be made up of savage, hostile tribes. All sorts of scary stories were told about them. They invoked magic spells against their enemies. They rolled rocks down from cliffs to crush them. They even forced their enemies to drink from a secret spring which had the power to make a person laugh so long and so hard that he became paralyzed. And since the Yis had in the past been treated badly by Nationalist soldiers, they took for granted that all soldiers were their enemies.

Certainly when the vanguard units entered the Yi territory on May 22, the people seemed to fit the stories told about them. Rushing down from the mountains, crowds of Yis, shouting their war cry, an eerie wolf-like "Whoo-oo-oo," blocked all passage on the road. They were armed with clubs, spears, rocks, and guns and made it clear that they would not allow any army to pass through their land. Fortunately, the Red Army had a man who could speak the Yi language, yet even he could not convince the Yis that the Red Army meant no harm. It was not until a top-ranking Yi, uncle of a Yi chief, rode up on his mule that the Yis were willing to listen. In the end, a Red officer, speaking through the interpreter, persuaded the uncle that his chief would like to become a blood brother of the Yi chief. Suddenly everyone became friendly. Chen Changfeng, who had worried about the fierceness of the Yis, couldn't get over how all at once the Yis were singing, giving away presents, laughing at everything and nothing, almost as if they had taken a sip from their secret spring.

The Yis had a ritual for becoming blood brothers. Their chief, his uncle, and the commanding Red officer went to a lake and filled two bowls with water. Then a cock (a common pet among the Yis) was brought to the spot, its beak broken off, and its blood spattered into the bowls. The Red officer and the Yi chief raised their bowls, entwining their right arms and holding them high. "To the Heavens above," the Red officer cried, "and the Earth below, I pledge to become the sworn brother to Xiau Yedan [the Yi chief]." He drank the blood-spattered water in one gulp while the Yi chief did the same. The Yi sealed the pledge. "If this oath be violated, may we die like chickens."

So the chicken-blood oath kept the Communist Army safe as it passed through the land of the Yi. Now if they would just have as much luck on the Dadu River! One Red Army general said that luck—plain luck—took much credit for whatever happened. "I believe in luck," he said. "You can't stop luck. You can't close a door on luck. And you can't bolt the door against it. It will always win out—if it is there." The big word was of course *if*, but it did seem that luck might be with the Red troops as they entered the first Chinese village beyond the Yi area.

It was night when the advance unit met an armed force of bandits who stopped them on the road. At first this did not seem particularly lucky, especially since the bandits had been organized by local landlords and were, as they proudly announced, working for the Nationalists. The lucky thing was that the bandits had never seen either Nationalist or Communist soldiers before and didn't know the difference. So here was another chance for the Red soldiers to pretend to be the enemy. Under cover of darkness they exchanged their caps for Nationalist caps and insignia they had captured at Zunyi. Then adopting the loud, aggressive tone typical of Nationalist soldiers, they demanded to see the district chief.

More luck. The district chief, according to one Communist soldier, was a "muddle-headed" man, easy to fool. He made a great fuss over the "Nationalist" soldiers, ordered an elaborate banquet for them, and then proceeded to give them information on the Dadu River. He told them what road to take, explained that all but one ferryboat had been destroyed but that this boat was docked at the village of Anshunchang, one of the few places the river could be crossed. When the Communist troops had eaten all the food they could eat and obtained all the news they needed, they tied up the muddle-headed man and his friends and set off for Anshunchang.

Long before they reached the river, the soldiers could hear it. Perhaps it was not haunted by 40,000 water devils, as it was said to be, but it was difficult to believe that water alone could make such a thundering noise. It was as if someone had suddenly pulled out a plug in mountains where centuries of snow and rain had accumulated—enough to make a dozen rivers—but instead a single river crashed pell-mell down a narrow river bed, banging against boulders, churning into whirlpools, whipping up such a racket, it all but drowned out the sound of an approaching army. Besides, the enemy, stationed on both sides of the river, had not been listening for an army. The Nationalists had not been expecting the Red Army to arrive so soon. Even so, the Red soldiers knew, battles would have to be fought—first at Anshunchang on the west shore and, if they could get across the river, then on the east shore. The first battle started with a rush and ended fairly quickly, giving the Communist Army control of that one ferryboat.

But what good was a single ferryboat in the dark of night

without a boatman experienced in dealing with this particular river? And how could one boat, no matter how many trips it made, transport a whole army to the other side? This wasn't the River of Golden Sands; they didn't have nine days and nine nights to make a crossing. Indeed, they had very little time, for even now the enemy was surely sending up reinforcements. Then they'd be caught in the same trap as those 40,000 heroes a hundred years before. They had perished just because their leader had dallied around, taking three days off to celebrate the birth of a son.

All night the Red Army worked. By morning they had rounded up eight boatmen, had placed their cannon at strategic spots on the riverside, had equipped each of seventeen volunteers with a submachine gun, a pistol, a broadsword, a dozen hand grenades, and work tools. At the last minute the volunteers were given a rousing pep talk which was meant to make them feel like heroes.

"Comrades," their leader shouted. "The lives of thousands of Red Army men depend on you. Cross resolutely and wipe out the enemy!"

Everyone cheered. It was nice to feel like heroes, and as it turned out, they were lucky heroes. In spite of a rain of bullets from the enemy, in spite of the wild, rolling boat ride, they managed to cross the river. Then, with the help of covering fire from their own men, they managed to wipe out the Nationalists on the farther shore. Two more boats were found, and as fast as they could make the round trip, they were sent back and forth to ferry the troops across.

It was obvious, however, that they could never get the whole army across. After the First Division had been safely landed on the eastern shore, Mao decided that the ferrying had to stop. The First Division would march north from there while the rest of the army would march north on the western side of the river. They would meet ninety miles away at the only other place where it was possible to cross the Dadu River—Luding Bridge. In the entire army no one had ever crossed Luding Bridge except Zhu De, but everyone had heard of it. Iron chains and wooden planks flung from one cliff to another—that's what Luding Bridge was, and the fate of China depended now on whether any army could cross it. Or if the bridge was even still there. Perhaps the Nationalists had destroyed it. They had a fort and a large contingent of men guarding the bridge on the far shore and they were expecting more momentarily. So of course it was important for the Red Army to beat the Nationalist reinforcements to Luding.

No one was surprised that Yang Chengwu was the one selected to lead the shock troops up the river and over the bridge. His whole army career had been spent on the run and now he was given three days (from May 27 to May 30) to cover ninety miles of mountain paths that wriggled and twisted, Yang said, like a "sheep's gut." Yang had been wounded again in his leg so for the first day and night he rode a horse, but when in the early morning of the second day he received orders to quicken the pace and arrive at the bridge not on May 30 but on May 29—the very next day—he dismounted from his horse. How could Yang Chengwu ask his men to walk sixty-five to seventy miles in twenty-four hours while he rode a horse? Everyone urged him to ride but he refused. "On to Luding!" he shouted as he joined the ranks. "Let's see who can get there first."

Hardly had they started out on the morning of the twenty-eighth when they came to Fierce Tiger Ridge, a mountain that had to be climbed on a dangerous trail in a fog so thick no one could see five steps ahead. And at the summit a detachment of Nationalists was waiting for them. They didn't wait long enough to see the Red troops. Instead, as soon as they heard men approaching they began shooting into the fog. Blind shots that did little damage. Actually there was no way to shoot at that range except blindly, so the Red soldiers were ordered not to shoot back. Wait until they were close enough to the enemy, they were told; then use hand grenades and bayonets. So Yang Chengwu and his comrades crept forward silently and then suddenly jumped out of the fog, bayonets pointing, grenades exploding. Panic-stricken, the Nationalists turned and ran.

But nothing went easily. When the fog lifted, the rain came. Drenching rain that made the path so slippery the men cut staffs to help them keep their footing. When this failed, they took off their puttees and tied themselves together in a chain.

By evening the weather had cleared and the path, winding down from the mountain, was again beside the river. But the Red Army was not alone. On the other side of the river another army marched, keeping pace with the Reds, holding lighted torches in the dark. Yang Chengwu knew that their First Division on the other side of the river had been waylaid, so he realized that these must be enemy reinforcements. But did the enemy know who *they* were? He decided to take a chance that they didn't. He obtained reeds to use as torches and distributed them, one to each squad, so they would look like the marchers across the river, all part of the same army. Then he ordered a bugler to stand by, ready to answer the enemy in their own code if they should signal. (The Communists had learned the code from a captured bugler.) Yang also had a soldier from Sichuan ready to answer any questions shouted across the river in Sichuan dialect.

It worked out just as Yang Chengwu had hoped. When an enemy bugler sounded his call, the Reds answered. When a soldier from across the river cried, "Which unit are you?" the Sichuan man gave the number of the enemy unit the Reds had routed that day. With the river between them, the two armies marched side by side, but how could the Red soldiers hope to beat the enemy this way? They couldn't get ahead of the enemy and they couldn't expect help from their waylaid First Division on the other side of the river. Disheartened, the tired soldiers simply slogged on—walking, walking, walking, as if their bodies had forgotten how to do anything else.

At midnight, however, the enemy quit walking. When the Red soldiers looked across the river, they saw that the men over there were putting out their torches and making camp.

Here was their chance! Tired as they were, they couldn't help grinning and congratulating each other. They had fooled the enemy again. Now if they could just force themselves to stay awake and keep going, they would be at Luding Bridge at daybreak, long before the enemy reinforcements were even near. Already they had left behind everything that would slow them down—pack animals, heavy luggage, even Yang Chengwu's horse—but now, as they went on, they tossed aside knapsacks, food, anything not absolutely essential. They kept only their guns and ammunition with them. They walked in single file and talked only when necessary. If anyone showed signs of dozing off, the man behind would give him a push. "Keep walking," he'd say.

At six o'clock in the morning, right on schedule, the Red soldiers finally reached Luding Bridge. Yes, the bridge was still there. Limping painfully, Yang Chengwu went to look at it. It was just as it had been described. One hundred twenty yards wide with two thick iron chains that served as hand-railings and nine chains laid lengthwise to support a plank floor. But the planks were not there. Obviously they had been removed by the enemy, and for two-thirds of the way across the bridge there were only chains that lay bare with wide gaps between them. Under the chains the Dadu River tossed and tumbled even more fiercely than it had at Anshunchang. Looking down, Yang Chengwu said he didn't see how even a fish could keep steady, let alone stay alive, in a current like that.

On the other side of the river stood the town of Luding, protected by strong fortifications with machine-gun emplacements close to the bridge. A group of enemy soldiers stood laughing.

"Come on!" they shouted. "Let's see you fly over."

Yang Chengwu was a young man with a trim figure, a tight, determined face, eyes that could flash fiercely one moment and in the next crinkle up with laughter. But no one who had met Yang Chengwu would forget his hands, for they were constantly in motion, underlining his words, giving shape to his emotions. Now he went back to his men and his hands went to work as he began issuing orders which had to be fulfilled before the battle for the bridge could begin. Occasionally the enemy lobbed mortar shells across the river, but the Reds were too busy to pay much attention.

Food had to be found and prepared, since men could not fight well on empty stomachs. Wood. Any kind, every kind of wood must be obtained. Doors from houses, fences. Trees must be cut into logs. After the first wave of fighters had crawled across those bare chains, a second wave would have to lay down a flooring so the rest of the army could march across.

The most important work, however, was preparing the men. From company to company, Yang Chengwu went, giving hero talks that had his voice ringing and his hands taking off with an excitement all their own. It may have seemed impossible to do what he was asking, yet when he had finished talking, the men were begging to be among those picked to crawl over the bare chains.

It was four o'clock in the afternoon before they were ready to begin battle. The buglers blew the call to charge, the gunners opened fire, and as everyone shouted encouragement, the twenty-two volunteers edged their way onto the chains. Swords and guns were strapped to their backs, grenades hung at their belts as they inched forward, link by link, holding to the handrail while they tried desperately to keep their footing on the chain below. Not for one moment could they let themselves be distracted, not when the enemy's bullets whizzed by their heads, not even when a bullet struck one of their comrades and they heard his body splash into the river. Four times they heard a splash but the eighteen survivors concentrated only on where to put their hands next, where to move their feet. Behind them came Yang Chengwu, leading those who were laying logs and improvised planking across the chains. Bending low, firing as they moved ahead, they also had to watch every step with care.

Zhu De stood on the bank where the bridge started. He was like stone, not a muscle moving. Seldom did anyone see him without a smile on his face but there was no smile now. Everything, *everything* depended on what happened here.

The first group had almost reached the place where the enemy had left the planks still in place, when suddenly they heard shouting from their shore. Glancing ahead, they saw Nationalist soldiers moving onto those planks and pouring kerosene on them. In the next minute the planks were in flames.

Yang Chengwu shouted to those ahead. "Charge in!" he called. "Don't be afraid! Charge in! The enemy is crushed. Charge!"

The bugles blew and the volunteers did charge. They crouched and ran fast, and with their hands free now, they threw hand grenades into the smoke. One man had his cap set on fire but he and the others made it safely over the planks to the riverbank. Those following stamped out the fire and immediately the rest of the troops marched over the swaying bridge to join in the battle on the other side.

Often it is not just superior fighters who win battles; it is those who care most deeply, those who have a cause more important to them than their own lives. The Red soldiers were so passionate about their program to save China that if they failed, they felt, it would be not just the defeat of an army but a defeat for China. If they failed, the peasants who put their faith in the Revolution would simply give up. So the soldiers threw themselves heart and soul into every battle and within a few hours at Luding they had taken the city and had sent the Nationalists running.

Still, they had to be ready for those reinforcements they knew were coming. At ten o'clock that evening the reinforcements seemed to be arriving, but when Yang Chengwu's men advanced, they discovered that this was not the enemy after all. These men were their own, from the First Division which had crossed on the ferry and marched up the other side of the river. They had overtaken the Nationalist reinforcements, fought them, and defeated them. As the two groups met and mingled, there was much shouting and cheering, for now their victory was complete.

Carrying a lantern, Yang Chengwu accompanied two of the leaders of the First Division to inspect Luding Bridge. At the middle of the bridge, one of the leaders, General Liu, stopped. Holding the chain handrail, he looked over the side to the raging waters below. He tapped his foot on a wooden plank as if he were making sure it was really there. "We've got you, Luding Bridge," he whispered. "We paid a great price, but we got you. We won out."

The next day the main army reached the bridge and crossed. The final group to arrive included Mao Zedong and his bodyguards. While soldiers on both sides of the river cheered the arrival of Mao, other officers rushed across the bridge to welcome him and escort him across.

Chen Changfeng stayed close behind Mao as he stepped on the bridge. He tried hard to feel like a hero but instead he suddenly felt like a little boy, not even a brave little boy. The bridge was so high and between the planks he could see the river rushing and rumbling below. If a person didn't step carefully, he could fall between the planks and be gone forever. Chen could imagine exactly how it would feel to fall, yet when he looked ahead, there was Mao, stepping along jauntily as if he were walking down a road in Jiangxi Province.

Mao turned toward Chen. "Scared?" he asked.

Chen was far too scared to answer. He shook his head. No. But by the time they were halfway across, the bridge was swaying so much that Chen's head was going around in circles and he had to stop and hold on to the handrail. Mao stopped and, reaching back, he took Chen's hand.

"Don't look down," Mao said as together they walked hand in hand to the other side of the bridge.

Here a feast was ready to celebrate what was surely the army's most daring exploit. Rice, pumpkin, potatoes—these were a treat for men who had no more than an occasional morsel of rice to swallow as they walked. Now they could eat hot food, sing, laugh, and marvel at their victory. And there were gifts. Twenty-four men, including Yang Chengwu, were pronounced heroes and each received a tunic with three buttons, a fountain pen, a notebook, an enamel bowl, and a pair of chopsticks made of imitation ivory.

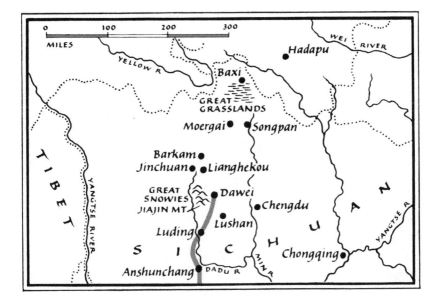

SIX ⸬ When the soldiers left the area of Luding Bridge, they knew that their immediate purpose was to meet up with Zhang Guotao and the Fourth Front Army. Although the two armies had lost touch with each other, for some reason which is still unclear, Mao Zedong was sure that the Fourth Front Army was only about a hundred miles north. But how were they going to get there? The men did not have to go far before they could see that the way north was blocked by mountains. And such mountains! Who would believe that mountains could fling themselves so far into the heavens? Chen Changfeng said they were "weird." And no wonder. This was June, yet the tops of those mountains were covered with snow. They were always covered with snow, he was told. The snow had been there for thousands of years and never melted. Southerners,

75

who had little experience with cold weather, could not imagine how it would feel to walk in snow that was thousands of years old. Surely no army, even for the sake of the Revolution, would be asked to do that.

The mountains were called the Great Snowies and when the army reached the base, Chairman Mao stopped. There were three ways the army might go. One road led to the west of the mountains but Tibetans lived there and were known to be fierce and warlike. One road led to the east of the mountains, to areas known to be occupied by the Nationalists. And there was one little rough path that went straight north across the mountains. Perhaps Mao had already decided how to go; perhaps only now he made up his mind. They would go straight north, he said. They wouldn't follow the curve of the bowl this time but would cut right through. Up and over. It may have been the logical choice. Still, Mao always seemed to be testing himself and the army as if he had to prove that nothing should be too hard for revolutionaries.

First, however, they stopped beneath the mountains to rest and prepare for the ordeal that lay ahead. They were supposed to take a ten-day supply of food with them. Most important for fighting the cold, the cooks were told to take ginger for the soldiers to chew and hot peppers to make hot-pepper soup. Mao Zedong, who came from Hunan Province, where hot, spicy food was popular, used to joke about the soup. No one could be a true revolutionary, he laughed, if he didn't like hot-pepper soup. Some of the officers who came from other provinces didn't think this joke was so funny. They were true revolutionaries and they didn't care for hot-pepper soup.

Clothes were another concern. Now that it was summer, many of the men had only thin cotton suits. They were down to one pair of worn sandals and sometimes went barefoot or wrapped their feet in rags. When a group of Tibetan warriors suddenly appeared on horseback, the soldiers fell on them. It wasn't the men that they were so glad to capture. It was their clothes and their horses. The Tibetan soldiers had sheepskin coats; their officers had fur-lined coats and the women had coats with fur on the outside. The horses were proud, well fed, and spirited.

The Communist women admired those horses. Mules and horses, they joked, were more valuable than husbands because husbands were easier to replace. As for the warm coats, they couldn't begin to go around even when they took turns wearing them, but they did make a difference to the few who had a turn. Kang Keqing was so cold she had trouble going over the first mountain, but when she went over the second mountain, she wore a fur coat and managed quite well.

For ten days the army stayed in fields of flowers, soaking up the sunshine as they worked on mending their clothes and weaving new straw sandals. Each man was to take two pair of shoes with him but not many were as lucky as one young soldier who had been given a pair of cloth shoes when he left Jiangxi Province. He considered them to be lucky shoes, his "seven-league boots," and he kept them tied to his belt during most of the March, waiting for an emergency. At Zunyi an enemy bullet which might have wounded him had instead gone through one of his shoes, leaving a small hole. This proved, he said, that the shoes were lucky and now it looked as if that emergency might be just ahead.

One of the advantages of having this long rest period was that the soldiers could get used to looking at the mountains. The most fearsome mountain was the closest, Jiajin, or Fairy Mountain, 16,000 feet high. Chen Changfeng said that its peak "pierced the sky like a sword point glittering in the sunlight." At times it would disappear behind clouds of snow that "swirled around the peak like a vast umbrella." Local people said the mountain was too high even for birds to fly over and too high for men to climb. They told of villagers who tried to cross and never came back. Indeed, if a man reached the top and opened his mouth, they said, the God of the Mountain would choke him to death. Only the Immortals could fly over.

Chairman Mao scoffed at such talk. The Red Army should have the courage to compete with the Immortals. In any case, the mountains had to be crossed and the army must learn how to survive at high altitudes where the air was thin. To conserve their energy, the men must walk slowly but steadily and talk only in whispers. They must loosen their clothing so they could breathe more easily. They must carry a cloth to shade their eyes so they wouldn't be blinded by the brilliant reflections of sun on snow. And they must keep going. Anyone who sat down even for a moment was apt to freeze before he could get back on his feet.

The prospect was alarming, but the propaganda team made up songs and had all the soldiers singing to keep their courage high. Even if they couldn't sing as they climbed, they should learn the words and think of them.

> *Jiajin Mountain is very high;*
> *You must not stop.*
> *Wrap your feet and rub them well—*
> *Don't rest at the top.*
> *You must climb and climb and climb;*
> *All must do the same.*
> *Help those who may be sick.*
> *Help those who may be lame.*

There may have been games and entertainment to divert them while they rested and the women may have served, as they often did, what they called "mental meals." Groups would squat down with their bowls and chopsticks and take turns describing a favorite dish from their hometown. There would be much laughing at these pretend-feasts as they competed, each trying to make his or her dish sound tastier than any other. Also they would spend time, as they did at every rest period, going after their fleas. They all had fleas. They picked them up from sleeping on the ground and kept them simply because it was impossible to keep their bodies clean. Liu Ying said that during the whole march she never once took off all her clothes. So they'd unbutton their jackets and go on flea hunts. "Go after them," Mao would say. "They're not worth keeping. Throw them away." Years later when she remembered those fleas, Liu Ying laughed. "It was fun to crack them," she said.

They finally started up the mountain one foggy morning just as the night sky was fading into gray. At first the mountain seemed as familiar as any mountain. They walked on dead leaves and stepped over fallen branches and rotten tree trunks. Above them birds, waking up to a June day, sang as if they lived in a private forest that went on forever. Gradually, however, trees became scarcer and stopped. The birds and their songs were left behind. The soldiers were entering what they had begun to think of as the world of the sleeping white tiger.

An artillery soldier in Yang Chengwu's unit pulled a handful of paper circles from his jacket, placed them on the ground, and set them afire. Yang Chengwu knew what he was doing. He was the superstitious soldier who had joined the Red Army after being captured from the Nationalists. The round pieces of paper were supposed to represent round silver dollars and he was making an offering to the God of the Mountain. The smoke was supposed to ascend like a prayer. As the soldier bowed low before the fire, Yang Chengwu laughed at him and his old-fashioned foolishness.

"You'll see," the soldier replied. "If you don't make an offering, you won't get across."

There is no record whether the superstitious soldier managed better than others or even if he did get across. Certainly he suffered. They all did. At first Zhou Enlai's bodyguard, Wei Guolu, felt excited about being in a world of snow. Like the others, he had cut himself a walking stick and planned to use it when the path became dangerous. But he and his comrades made one mistake. They should never have imagined that the white tiger was sleeping. Within moments the snow was attacking them from all sides, whirling around their bent bodies, piling up at their feet. Only snow that was thousands of years old could be so cold, they decided. Only wind that came down from such heights could be so fierce.

One of the little red devils, seeing himself enclosed in a world of white, supposed he was in the sky. "We're walking on the clouds, aren't we?" he asked an officer.

At first it was the depth of the snow that made each step so difficult. Then the snow froze into ice and as the army proceeded in single file, those in front used their bayonets to dig footholes for those who followed. Everyone joined hands and all that could be heard on the mountain was the clacking of walking sticks as the men tried to find solid footing. From time to time a man would fall like a tree and lie where he had fallen like dead wood. When a friend from Wei Guolu's hometown fell, Wei rushed to help him, but by the time he had leaned over, his friend was dead.

Chen Changfeng worried about Chairman Mao. In the thin cotton suit that he wore, he bent forward, his shoulders hunched, and for every three or four steps forward he would slip back a step. Chen and Mao's other bodyguards tried to help. "Chairman," Chen said. "Lean on us. Let us support you." But Mao said no. They should just take care of themselves.

In the early afternoon the snow turned into a hailstorm and they felt that they were back at war. The hailstones were like cannonballs bombarding them so relentlessly, it was impossible to make any progress. Mao's bodyguards quickly raised an oilskin sheet over him and together they huddled

beneath it, listening to the thundering of the storm, the neighing of frightened horses, the rattling and bouncing of hailstones on ice.

Just as quickly as the storm started, it stopped. Mao stepped out of his oilskin shelter. "Well, how did we come out of that battle?" he asked. "Anyone wounded?"

No one was wounded, but it was so cold that the air the soldiers breathed froze on their faces, giving them all white beards. Many had wrapped quilts around their shoulders or waists, but their hands and lips were blue. Chen was so short of breath, he had increasing trouble with every step. All at once he became dizzy and his legs trembled in a strange way that he didn't understand. "Chairman," he whispered, but before he could say any more, he collapsed in the snow. Mao raised him up and, as Chen said, he felt as if he were swimming in space. In a few moments, however, Chen's head cleared and when he tried out his legs, he found they worked.

Chen was luckier than many, luckier than some of the happy-go-lucky cooks who thought nothing could happen to them. In many of the companies the men took turns cooking or, as they said, "being parents to the others." But some companies had men permanently assigned as cooks. The nine cooks assigned to one particular company took it upon themselves not only to keep the men fed but to keep them in good humor. They would go through all kinds of antics to get a laugh, sometimes clowning as they chased each other, their pots and pans clanking at their sides. They became known as the "theater troupe," and before going up the Snowies, they bragged that they would not let a single man die. Although no one was supposed to carry more than forty pounds up the mountains, the cooks put extra food in their pots so that each one was carrying seventy or eighty pounds. They did not go through any antics but they did hurry. They arrived at the top of the mountain ahead of the soldiers and had hot-pepper soup ready for them.

Some men were so tired when they reached the top, they dropped to the ground. Their minds had become muddled in the thin air and they no longer cared what happened. As they began slipping into unconsciousness, the cooks rushed from one to another, trying to revive them, trying to force hot soup into their mouths. But it was too late. It was even too late for two of the cooks. They died, soup bowls still in their hands.

Perhaps most men were too weary to notice the group of small ragged homemade flags flying on sticks propped up by stones at the top of the mountain. But Ding Ganru noticed. He was the little red devil who had held on to a horse's tail while crossing the Xiang River. Horses' tails had come in handy throughout the March. Even up this mountain some had clung to them, but Ding had managed on his own and he was proud of it. He knew that these little flags had been put there by local people to thank the God of the Mountain for letting them cross. He didn't feel like thanking any mountain god but he did think those little flags had a brave, triumphant look about them. He would like to have flown his own flag just to celebrate the climb, but he had nothing he could fly. Still, he did feel triumphant.

Now they had to get down from the mountain. Since Ding was in the rear guard, he didn't need to wonder how they would manage. He could hear the soldiers shouting and see what they were doing. They were sliding down. It was as if they had suddenly been let out of school for recess as they scooted down the mountain on their backsides. It was not good for their backsides but it was quick and at the bottom the weather was warm again.

In the valley there was time for a short rest but not much time since they had to watch their food supply. Rice was not grown in this area, only highland barley. Many men could not digest the barley and of course, weak as they were, they became weaker. The army was dwindling and so exhausted that when they finally reached a village where they could buy food, Mao decided that the main forces should rest for a week while a vanguard unit went ahead and looked for the mysterious Fourth Front Army.

For two days the vanguard marched but the only people they saw were hostile tribesmen who stood on cliffs and rolled boulders down on them. Although they managed to dodge the boulders, still it was not pleasant to hear the eerie "wong-g wong-g" noise that the tribesmen's horns made as they called to one another. Then suddenly on the hills they noticed a column of men running toward them. More tribesmen? They were shouting as they ran, but the vanguard, in the midst of building a pontoon over a river, couldn't figure out what they were saying. The river was making so much noise that no words came through. A few of the men on the mountain began throwing stones, not big ones, and for some reason there seemed to be nothing unfriendly in what they were doing. Puzzled, a soldier in the vanguard picked up one of the stones and saw that it was wrapped in paper. On the paper was written a name. As soon as he read it, the soldier let out a whoop. They all knew that name. It belonged to a general in the Fourth Front Army. Then from the mountain came a familiar Red Army bugle call.

All the soldiers began shouting, waving their arms, hugging each other. This was the Fourth Front! Two generals were lowered by rope from the mountain and General Peng Dehuai, the general with the vanguard, ran to meet them. Peng had never wept over physical hardship or over fallen friends, but now, along with others in the vanguard, he wept. No longer was the First Front Army alone.

This reunion took place just outside the village of Dawei on June 12. On June 14, after Mao and the remaining forces of the First Front Army had arrived in Dawei, a celebration was held. Perhaps the best part was the huge feast provided by the Fourth Front, which was well supplied with food—

yak meat, mutton, potato flakes, corn mush, and barley (which many may have chosen to pass up). Or perhaps the best part was the unrestrained fun they had around the bonfires. Li Bozhao, a general's wife known for her theatrical ability, danced a Russian sailor's dance with such verve that no one wanted her to stop. They all sang—Communist songs, folk songs, and a favorite sung to the tune of "Row, Row, Row Your Boat." At the end they may all have danced what they called the "Poor Man's Dance"—dancing without music.

This was not, however, an official reunion. Since Zhang Guotao and many of his men were still far away, the First Front and the Fourth Front were scheduled to meet officially on June 25 at a town thirty miles north of Dawei. Meanwhile there were a few more Snowies to cross, mountains with names like Dream Pen Mountain and Big Drum Mountain and one mountain so high that Nationalist planes couldn't reach the top. Seeing the pilot in the cockpit of a Nationalist plane flying below, the Red soldiers waved to him. "Come on up!" they called.

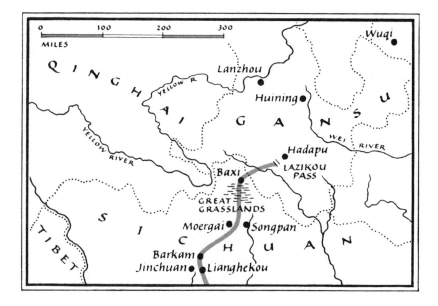

SEVEN

Perhaps even before the big reunion of June 25, the survivors of the First Front Army wondered about their new comrades in the Fourth. Although they had met only a small number, it was easy to see that they were better fed, better dressed, and that they had lived easier lives. And what about their commander, Zhang Guotao? Some said that Zhang was kind to his men. Some said that he was so suspicious of spies within his army, he executed anyone about whom he had the slightest suspicion. Supposedly he had special agents whose job it was to talk to soldiers and report what was said. Even an innocent remark might be construed as disloyalty. The little red devils in the Fourth Front had a saying:

> *Heaven I don't fear; Earth I don't fear.*
> *I just fear to talk when special agents are near.*

It had been a long time since First Front soldiers had had someone new to gossip about, but in the end, they agreed, what difference did it make to them what kind of man Zhang was? The important thing was that the two armies were together and they all felt stronger and ready to celebrate.

From one end to the other, the town of Lianghekou, where the First Front made its headquarters, was decorated in red in honor of the occasion. Red banners, red bunting, red flags festooned the streets and buildings. "Welcome! Welcome!" the banners proclaimed. Slogans were painted on the walls. "Long Live the Red Army!" A platform had been set up in a field outside of town where the official ceremony was to be held. Preparations were made for a feast. Huge vats of soup, rice, chicken, and pork were all in the making. Moreover, soldiers of the First Front were doing their best to make themselves more presentable. They had been far too busy just trying to survive to notice that their hair had grown long and scraggly or that their uniforms were torn. But now they would be on exhibit before the Fourth so they spruced up as much as they were able.

The actual meeting of the two commanders was to take place on the road about a mile outside of the town. Unfortunately it was raining on the twenty-fifth, but that did not keep crowds from the surrounding area from gathering to witness this historic event. As the time drew near, Mao was taken to an oilcloth tent on the roadside where he could wait for Zhang Guotao to arrive.

At five o'clock in the afternoon word passed through the crowd that horses were approaching. Troops on either side of the road snapped to attention. Mao Zedong stepped out of his shelter as Zhang Guotao, seated on a white horse and accompanied by a dozen mounted aides, rode up to Mao. Zhang jumped to the ground, and as the two commanders threw open their arms for a welcoming hug, the crowds cheered. Certainly there was every evidence of friendship as the two men walked to the ceremonial platform, their arms draped around each other's shoulders.

Later, when the First Front soldiers recalled their initial impressions, they would speak of the way Zhang's horses spattered mud right and left as they sprinted up the road, not stopping until they had been reined in at the last moment in front of Mao, patiently waiting on foot. Then, as Zhang's troops followed, how could the First Front men not notice that the caps of the Fourth were bigger than theirs? And the horses. Repeatedly Mao's army talked of how fat the Fourth Front Army's horses were. Imagine how much food the men must have if they could afford to give the horses so much! Overhearing their remarks, Mao smiled. "Don't envy the horses," he told his men.

But as time went on, it became clear that it was not the horses or the men causing trouble between the two armies. It was Zhang Guotao himself. Both Zhang and Mao were among the twelve original founders of the Communist Party in China in 1921, but in his own eyes Zhang obviously believed that he had become Mao's superior. Look at the size of the two armies. Neither Mao nor Zhang knew exactly how large the other army was, but anyone could see that the Fourth vastly outnumbered the First. (Actually, Mao was down to about 10,000 men, while in the relative safety of northwest Sichuan Zhang had built up an army of between 70,000 and 80,000, including a regiment of 2,000 women.) Zhang Guotao, a naturally jealous and arrogant man, considered his soldiers to be his personal army, so of course he didn't like the way those in the First Front Army seemed to take for granted that Mao was in charge of everything. In turn, the men in the First Front didn't like the way the Fourth Front men referred to Zhang Guotao as "Chairman." Nor did they like the way Zhang seemed to look down on them, sometimes almost in the manner of a landlord.

On the whole, however, the men in the First Front and the

Fourth Front Armies enjoyed each other's company, although they were aware of the growing tension between their leaders, who couldn't agree about where they should go from here. Even when they left Lianghekou, they were still arguing. Zhang wanted to move west and south to establish a route the Russians could use if they felt like helping, but Mao was against this. In such a remote area among minorities, he said, it would be hard to secure food, hard to get recruits, and most important, the Communist troops would lose touch with the rest of China. Mao wanted to go north and establish a base away from Tibetans; he wanted to be in an area populated by mainstream Chinese where the Red Army could spread its influence. Mao won the argument but Zhang sulked. Zhu De, who seemed to have won the confidence of Zhang Guotao, kept going back and forth between the two men, trying to smooth matters over.

But if the soldiers in the First Front Army wondered what was going on at the top, they forgot everything when they came down from the last of the Snowies and were taken by surprise to see what was there. All at once, in the middle of an empty plain, a tower rose up before them. Story upon story, it reached into the sky. They counted the stories. Seven in all. It must be a mirage, they thought—a castle out of a fairy tale suddenly appearing in the middle of nowhere. Moreover, it appeared to be empty. There were cannon emplacements in the thick wall surrounding the castle but no one was shooting cannon at them. There were openings in the wall for archers but no arrows appeared. There was no activity at all. Obviously this must be the headquarters of a rich and powerful Tibetan chief and, like all Tibetans in this part of China, he must have fled when he heard that the Red Army was coming. And no wonder. The Tibetans believed the horror stories that the Nationalists had told them. Communists liked to steal Tibetan babies and eat them, the Nationalists said, so of course even a Tibetan chief grabbed up his babies and ran when he heard the Communists were on their way. The other occupants of the castle ran with him.

So there was nothing to stop the First Front Army soldiers (who were a day ahead of the Fourth Front) from walking right into the castle and making themselves at home. Chen Changfeng would have been in raptures. If the wealthy home in Zunyi had impressed him, the entrance alone of this place would have seemed overwhelming. Up and up it went, up all seven stories of the tower. Fancy carved balconies hung at every level. Columns lacquered in green, red, and black stood around the walls. Surely Chen Changfeng wasted no time in finding the chief's bedroom and presenting it to Mao as if it were a gift manufactured out of his own dreams. Here was a bed made of teakwood; here a desk of red lacquer. And if Mao wanted, he could pin his maps right on top of the tapestry that hung on the walls.

There was room in the castle and its outbuildings and grounds for the whole First Front Army to stay, but they didn't stay long. Still, they must have stayed long enough for the cooks to make use of the kitchen which occupied the entire first floor. And how those cooks would have carried on to have been turned loose in that kingdom of stoves! How they would have laughed to see all the brass and copper pots and pans and kettles at their disposal! The second floor was the storeroom for food, and although Tibetans did not usually leave food behind, in this case there was more than they could take with them; so the cooks would have had a chance to prepare a meal more tasty, more elaborate than any of the "mental meals" they had imagined on the March. Food had become a problem in this area. The army couldn't buy it and although they may have left IOUs for what they took (which they generally did), they were forced to become less strict about payment. The cooks would not have quibbled about helping themselves to what they found.

Although a few units of the army stayed behind so they

could pack the food from the castle and bring it along, the main force marched ahead to the town of Moergai, lying on the edge of a mysterious area called the Great Grasslands. It was rumored that these grasslands would be the most perilous ground the troops had yet crossed, but in any case they would rest for a month in Moergai before setting out. On the way they passed one deserted village after another, empty not only of people but also of food. Still, the army had to eat. Luckily the Tibetans fled before they had harvested and their wheat and barley stood tall and ripe in the fields. So the First Front Army moved north and cut the grain as they went. Zhu De, swinging a scythe, walked through fields, laughing and challenging anyone to cut and carry as much as he did. Kang Keqing, scythe in hand, was at his side accepting the challenge.

It was dangerous, however, to move too far away from others in the fields. Tibetan farmers were hidden close enough to their farms so they could leap out and kill a solitary figure before the rest would miss him. Sheep presented the greatest threat. How could a soldier, hungry for meat, resist the temptation of chasing a stray sheep even if the sheep led him away from his comrades? As many men were killed trying to capture sheep, it was said, as there were sheep actually captured.

It took ten days to reach Moergai, a town of about 400 stone houses, all empty. Small white ragged flags hung on the ends of poles at each corner of each house. As they flapped in the wind, the flags were supposed to carry the prayers of the homeowners to the gods above, but the prayers were not strong enough to keep the Red Army from moving into the houses and settling in the surrounding area.

Meanwhile the argument between the leaders went on and Zhang Guotao became increasingly bitter. It was power, of course, that Zhang wanted, and Zhu De finally figured out a way in which Zhang's pride would be saved and they could still march north. They would march in two columns, Zhang on the western side of the Grasslands and Mao on the eastern side. Some of the Fourth Front Army would march with the First; some of the First would go with the Fourth. Zhu De would go with Zhang and be overall commander in chief while Zhang would be the chief political commissar. Zhang's column would have 30,000 troops; Mao's would have about 9,000. Mao was agreeable. After all, the important thing was that the two columns would meet north of the Grasslands and the army would stay united. And since Zhu De would be with the western column, he could keep a close watch on Zhang.

With that settled, Mao turned his attention to the Grasslands. This was another challenge, even greater than the Snowies, for no one—certainly not the Nationalists— would expect an army to be so foolhardy as to enter this terrible wasteland of swamps and quicksand. On August 17 Mao decided it was time to give specific instructions to the vanguard unit. He sent for Yang Chengwu, whose regiment was stationed some miles away. Generally Yang received his orders from his immediate superior, but this time Mao wanted to give them personally.

When Yang received the summons, he could barely contain his excitement. A private conference! Orders directly from the Chairman! He jumped on his horse and galloped as fast as he could, yet it didn't seem fast enough. When he arrived at headquarters in Moergai, Yang leaped off his horse, smoothed out his uniform, and at the door of Mao's room, he announced his presence in his loudest, most military voice.

Chairman Mao was at his desk, looking at a map. "Well, here you are!" he said. He pointed to a wooden stool. "Sit down, sit down."

Yang lowered himself to the edge of the stool.

Mao smiled. "Well, again your regiment has been chosen,"

he said. "You will be the advance unit as we go into the Grasslands."

Yang jumped to his feet as though he were ready to start out right then, but as Mao pointed to the map Yang sat down again. The Grasslands were treacherous, Mao explained. Not only did a person not know where to put his feet, he did not know what direction to go. There were no trees, no landmarks of any kind, and if it wasn't foggy, it was raining, snowing, or hailing. The sky played all its tricks on the Grasslands. Yang would need a guide, Mao said.

Yang had anticipated this. Eagerly he told Mao about the sixty-year-old Tibetan who spoke a little Chinese with whom he had managed to make friends.

Sixty years old. Mao shook his head. What if the guide could not walk that far?

No problem, Yang replied. He'd be carried on a stretcher.

Mao listed all the preparations that Yang should make. In particular, he should have his soldiers equipped with wooden sticks marked "This Way" and with arrows pointing the way ahead for those behind to follow. "Be sure to make them steady," Mao said. He didn't want any wobbly arrows pointing the wrong way.

It was the middle of August when Yang's regiment came to the Grasslands. Yang pulled up his horse and took out his binoculars. As far as he could see in every direction, it was the same. Dead, empty, flat, with a low fog hanging over it all. Every living thing—birds, insects, trees—all had abandoned the place as if it were unfit for life. There was only grass and stagnant water that looked, one soldier said, like horses' urine and smelled worse. If ever a landscape could look evil, this one did. Deliberately evil, as if it preferred death and would resist any form of life at all.

Yang Chengwu put away his binoculars and looked helplessly at the Tibetan guide who was standing at his side. Where was the path? Yang wanted to know.

There was no path, the guide said. You simply followed the thickest grass roots, stepping from one to another, and they would take you north. So they started. The men were loaded down more heavily than usual, for each carried a marker as well as a bundle of firewood. They knew they would find no wood in this desolation and at the end of the day they would need a fire for cooking and for warmth. For comfort too. The night would seem less dark and the space less lonely with a fire burning.

But they were just starting out. They had not learned all the sky's tricks yet. They didn't know that it would rain—pour and rain—before it was time to build a fire, and it might keep on raining all night long. Now they were simply stepping from one clump of grass to another, trying to get used to the spongelike feeling underfoot and the mud making a squishing sound, *pu-chi, pu-chi*, every time they tried to pull their sandals free. Many times they did not pull them free, and as time went on, many men could not even pull themselves free. One misstep and the watery quicksand would suck a man under and he'd be gone forever.

In the middle of the afternoon the sky started to show off. It didn't begin with anything that could be called a trick; it was a total performance. The whole sky simply turned into water and hurled itself at the ground. At the same time the temperature fell. Although the Grasslands were flat, the elevation was high, so the army had expected cold but not such sudden teeth-chattering cold. Still, they slogged on as best as they could until dusk when the rain stopped.

Yang's first concern was for the guide. Fortunately they found a mound where they pitched a tent for him. The others would have to sleep in the open but they had counted on a fire. But how could they start a fire? The wood they'd been carrying was soaking wet. At least most of it. Seventeen-year-old Zheng Jinyu was a friend of Yang's, lively and full of fun like Yang's other young friend who had been killed at

Loushan Pass. Grinning, Zheng came forward, opened his jacket, and from under his arms he pulled some dry kindling, enough to coax a fire along. Always effusive, Yang would have laughed and shown his delight and pride in his friend. Indeed, everyone recognized that Zheng was the hero of the day.

They may all have thought that the worst was over as they drank the water boiled over the fire, mixing it with a little dry barley. But on the Grasslands it was dangerous ever to think that the worst was over. They had scarcely finished their barley water when a wind sprang up, bringing with it sheets of rain mingled with hailstones. A few of the men had brought oilpaper umbrellas but they not only did no good, they looked silly—flimsy little paper circles raised against such wildness. Since there was no shelter, the men sat together all night in small groups, their backs against each other to spread whatever warmth their bodies held.

There were worse times ahead. Once, after a rainstorm, they took off all their clothes, wrung them out, and put them on again. Until the next storm they would rather be simply wet than wet and dripping. One night there were so many puddles, they stood up the entire night, back to back. Their food began to give out. When they could count the grains of barley left in their bags, they picked grass and roots which they hoped were edible. Sometimes they were edible; sometimes they weren't. In any case, more and more men became sick. Zheng Jinyu, the firewood hero, was so ill he told Yang Chengwu that his legs were giving out.

"Politically I am as strong as a piece of iron," he said, "but I may not be able to make it."

Yang found some extra food for him and gave him his horse to ride. Then when Zheng became too weak to sit up, Yang had quilts put under him and tied him to the horse. But in the end Zheng truly couldn't make it. Yang tried to encourage him but Zheng knew it was no use. "I really can't

make it, Commissar," he said. "I really can't." Tears welled up in his eyes. "When the Revolution succeeds," he whispered, "will you tell my family that I died for it?"

Later, when Yang stood beside the body of his young friend, he was filled with anger at the Grasslands. It had no mercy. Not even for a happy young man who was so eager to live.

The rest of the column followed a few days behind the vanguard. They were a tatterdemalion group, many dressed in clothes too large, taken from landlords. Those who didn't have red-starred caps wore wide handmade hats of pleated bamboo, straw, or oilcloth. They looked, as one soldier put it, like an army of mushrooms on the march. They had the advantage of being able to follow the markers the vanguard had left behind, but in walking they were at a disadvantage. The vanguard had tramped down the grass clumps so they had to step even more gingerly than those who had gone ahead. Actually their feet were in mud most of the time, and at the end of the day, if they could find a dry spot, they would have to scrape their feet or the mud would cake and they wouldn't be able to walk. This was a job in which the little red devils were asked to help.

But food was their most serious problem. The vanguard had already pulled up anything that looked edible so there was little or nothing left to eat. Some became so hungry that they ate handfuls of wild grass even though they'd been told it was bad for them. Zhou Enlai caught one of his orderlies who had sneaked off by himself to be sick.

"What's the matter? Are you sick?" Zhou asked.

"No, I'm not."

"If you're not sick, then why did you vomit?"

After the orderly admitted he'd eaten the grass, Zhou gave him a bit of his own barley and reminded him to obey orders in the future.

One of the reasons the soldiers became so weak was that

they had no salt in their diet. Some of the women remembered the time earlier in the March when Kang Keqing had stopped a group of soldiers carrying what she thought was a large rock. Didn't they have enough to carry? she asked. What did they want with a rock? It was not a rock, she was told; it was a cake of salt. Years later they would still smile at Kang Keqing's surprise to find that salt came in that form. But there was no salt now and the water they drank was not clean. Liu Ying would fill a mug with water, let the bugs settle on the bottom, then transfer the water to another mug. This way, she could pretend the bugs had never been there.

At one point they became so desperate for food that they shot some of their horses, but of course there wasn't enough horse meat to go around. Then they began boiling leather belts, leather harnesses, and leather shoes which a few people had. They added some wild herbs they knew were safe and they ate this concoction, pretending it was a special treat. Zhou Enlai called it "Soup of Three Delicacies."

It took about a week to cross the Grasslands but it seemed a lifetime. It was as if the soldiers were on another planet and they hardly knew who they were. In China people grow up in small spaces, in the midst of large families, with neighbors nearby and pigs underfoot. Every morning starts off with roosters crowing and wells creaking. People do their living in the open—play games, prepare food in doorways, wash clothes in streams, call to each other from field to field. The terrible emptiness of the Grasslands was not just different—the Grasslands struck at their understanding of what life was.

When they finally emerged on a real path on hard ground, the first thing they noticed was stones. Stones! they cried. What could be more beautiful than stones? They picked them up, greeting them like old friends from a familiar world. Then in the distance they saw smoke rising from what must be a Tibetan village. Even the Tibetan guide got off his stretcher and joined in the general cheering. It was over! The terrible Grasslands, which had taken more of their men than the Snowies had, was finally behind them.

For some reason the Tibetans here were friendly to the Communist soldiers. As various units of the army straggled in over a succession of days, they were invited to share the houses in this village of Banyou and the nearby villages Axi and Baxi. They moved into the felt-covered huts of nomads or into more permanent houses with roofs made of dried yak dung, which they were surprised to find had no odor. The homes were primitive, many without windows, but they were warm and they were dry. The soldiers had hot water for washing their feet and when they went to sleep, they could stretch out their bodies and lie down full-length. As for food, there wasn't much, except rats. The villages were filled with rats, but when the Red Army left there were none. The men didn't complain; after all, a cooked rat was more nourishing than a boiled belt.

For a week they rested. Even Mao must have thought (or at least hoped) that their troubles were over. Of course he wondered how Zhang Guotao's western column was doing. On September 3 he heard. A radio message sent by Zhang stated that they had reached the White River but the river was flooded. They couldn't cross it. They would have to give up their plans for going north. Why didn't Mao's column recross the Grasslands and join them, he suggested. Then they could all go south together.

Mao found it hard to believe that they were stopped by a river. They *couldn't* cross it, he asked himself, or they *wouldn't?* He had no way of knowing that Zhu De had told Zhang that they could cross but Zhang had ignored him. Mao called a meeting of the leaders who agreed with Mao that this was a power play on Zhang's part to gain control of the entire army.

Mao sent Zhang a message urging him to stick to the original agreement made at Moergai. For the next week messages flashed back and forth. Once Mao offered to come and help Zhang cross the river, but for Zhang nothing would do but that they should all go south together. On September 9 Mao intercepted a message that Zhang sent to his most trusted officer, who was marching with Mao. In the message Zhang *ordered* Mao's whole column to come to him to work out their differences. Mao allowed the message to be delivered, never letting on that he had seen it. But late that night, on the pretext that the army needed to cut grain if they were to recross the Grasslands, he had his men on the move. North. He was worried about Zhang's message. What if those of the Fourth Front who were with him decided to *force* Mao and the men in the First Front to join Zhang? What if there was actually a fight? The Revolution would never survive if Communists began killing each other.

The First Front was well on its way before the men in the Fourth discovered what had happened. Mao stayed behind to address those who remained. He told them frankly that those who wanted to join Zhang and go south were free to go. Those who wanted to go north with him would be welcome.

So the men divided up according to their loyalties and their inclinations—some, obviously disheartened, back across the Grasslands; others north to join Mao's men. Mao prophesied that within a year the Fourth Front would join them but at the moment he was simply glad that the crisis was over. For a while it had seemed to him that all they had worked for might be lost. "It had been," he said later, "the darkest hour of my life."

But now the First Front Army (or all that was left of it) had to find a stopping place. They couldn't march forever. As far as anyone knew there was just one more obstacle, Lazikou Pass, before they would be back among their own people: Chinese-speaking Chinese. The pass was about two days away—a narrow point in the mountains (only twelve feet

102

wide at one place) with a river running far below between rocky cliffs. It was an ideal place to defend and, as Mao knew, Nationalist troops were already defending it.

Yang Chengwu and Wang Kaixiang, a fellow officer who had shared the dangers of so many advance assaults, were given orders on September 15 to get to Lazikou Pass as fast as possible. As usual, Yang gave his troops a rousing hero talk.

"Do you want to go back to the Grasslands?" he shouted.

With one voice the troops answered. "No!"

"We have surmounted the Snowies!" he cried.

The soldiers, making their hands into fists, shook their arms and shouted their agreement.

"We have taken Luding!"

More cheering.

"We have crossed the Grasslands. Are we going to let Lazikou stop us?"

"No!" The soldiers roared their response.

They started marching at eleven o'clock that night. At two in the morning of September 16 they stopped to eat and rest, and it may have been then that Wang Kaixiang did what he did every night of the March. He polished his pistol until it gleamed and he wound his gold watch—these were his two prized possessions. According to his watch, it was nine in the morning when the advance team actually started to assault the Nationalists at the pass, but Wang may have been too busy to consult his watch for some time. On the other hand, it was a long day and he may have looked at his watch again and again, wondering if the sun would ever set.

Nationalists were stationed on top of the opposite cliff. All they had to do was pour gunfire down on anyone who tried to cross the narrow bridge that led to the cliff. Still in full control of the pass at daybreak on September 17, they must have thought that they had at last stopped the Reds in their tracks; but at that very moment Red mountaineers were creeping behind them. Lashed together with their belts and puttees, they were climbing not only the cliff where the Nationalists were but the peak that rose above them. Once there, they unstrapped the hand grenades on their backs and hurled them down on the enemy. The whole cliff erupted in a battery of explosions and the Nationalists, those who had not been immediately killed, fled in all directions.

Lazikou Pass was open for the First Front Army to cross. It would take about a week for the army to reach the first Chinese village.

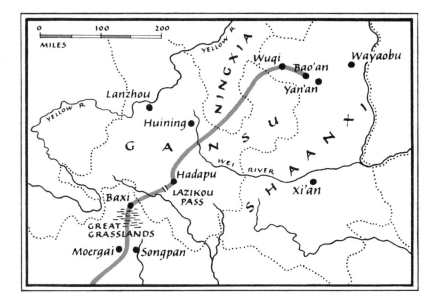

EIGHT

About two or three thousand people lived in the town of Hadapu. Alerted by Yang Chengwu's advance unit, they knew that the Red Army was coming, so they were ready. Banging gongs, beating drums, waving flags and banners, they all turned out to greet the soldiers as if they were heroes returning home to their families. And indeed the soldiers felt that they were home. Such a warmth of welcome! Such a crowd of real Chinese people speaking real Chinese that they could understand! Hadapu wasn't Jiangxi but suddenly it seemed almost like Jiangxi, and in a sudden burst of joy in being back with their own kind, the men found themselves hugging each other and everyone else in sight. Some even fell on their knees to kiss the ground. To celebrate, the leaders dug into that supply of silver dollars which had been carried over all the rivers,

105

over the mountains, and across the Grasslands. Each soldier was given two silver dollars and each soldier knew exactly what to buy.

Food. The people of Hadapu had laid in a great supply of food and Mao told the army to eat well. They began immediately. Did they want eggs? A dozen eggs sold for ten cents. One hundred pounds of vegetables cost fifty cents. Five chickens were a dollar; a sheep was two dollars; and if two men wanted to pool their money and persuaded a third man to contribute a dollar, they could buy a hundred-pound pig. They ate as if the food might disappear if they didn't eat fast enough. Indeed they gorged. Some men's stomachs became so full they burst and the men died. When the leaders saw what was happening, they ordered the soldiers to eat only a little, rest a while, eat a little more, then rest again. Still, it was hard to hold back after being starved for so long.

Hadapu had not only food but news. Had the troops been told the news, they would probably have celebrated even more, but Mao didn't tell them for another ten days, long after they'd left Hadapu. For the first time in months Mao had had a chance to see newspapers and he found out that in the next province, Shaanxi, there was a base where three other Communist armies had gathered. Together they had about the same number of men as Mao had in his own shrunken forces, down now to about 6,000.

At last Mao knew where they were going. Of course the first priority had always been to escape from the Nationalists and find a base where they could expand in safety. But Mao never forgot the long-range goals, nor did he let the army forget them. Eventually they had to beat the Nationalists, but they also had to get the Japanese out of China, which no one had succeeded in doing yet. The Japanese were a continuing military threat and everyone in China was anxious to get rid of them. "Go North and Fight the Japanese!" Red commanders had been using this slogan regularly in their hero talks. It was an inspiration to the troops and a rallying cry for the people in the countryside. Mao recognized the political advantage of appealing not only to the anti-landlord sentiments of the peasants but to the anti-Japanese sentiments as well. He may not have thought that this was a practical goal for the immediate future, but still it was a goal.

The troops, however, didn't need slogans or inspirational talks when they were told that now they had a destination. An end to their march. They found it hard to imagine—a real place where they could not only stop but also stay. And it was only 250 miles away.

There would still be a few skirmishes, particularly with regiments of Moslem cavalry fighting for the Nationalists. On October 20 at the town of Wuqi, Mao suggested that they rid themselves once and for all of this last stubborn group which continued to harass them. They would "cut off the tail" of the enemy, he said. So on the morning of the twenty-first Mao arranged his men in a half-circle which at the right moment could close in on the unsuspecting cavalry as they advanced. Mao had about 3,000 men assembled for battle; the enemy also had 3,000 but they were on horseback. It may have seemed that the enemy had the advantage, but as it turned out, those horses didn't want their tails cut off. Surrounded by gunfire, they couldn't get away fast enough. The battle was over in two hours.

Chen Changfeng, standing on a hilltop watching the retreat with Mao, burst out laughing. "Chairman," he said, "we've got only two legs and they have four but we have them running all over the mountain."

This was one battle, however, in which Yang Chengwu had no part. Nor did his fellow officer, Wang Kaixiang. Both had come down with typhoid fever and were simply too sick to move. Indeed, Wang was too sick to wind his watch at night, too sick to polish his pistol, and Yang was too sick to remind him. Yet Wang Kaixiang had not forgotten his pistol. As his fever mounted and mounted, he became delirious. He didn't know what he was doing but he did know that his beloved pistol lay under his pillow. He pulled it out and shot himself in the head. When Yang Chengwu recovered, he would mourn the loss of his friend as he mourned all losses.

The army stayed in Wuqi just three days, then moved on a short distance to Wayaobu, where Yang Chengwu rejoined his regiment. Now for the first time, a year later, the First Front Army could say that the Long March was over. Six thousand miles, from one end of China to the other. They had crossed twenty-four rivers, a thousand mountains, and marched through eleven provinces, losing thousands of men on the way. Yet they had to ask: How had any of them managed to survive? They could hardly understand it themselves.

Although their sense of brotherhood was strong, the First Front Army always felt an incompleteness in their group. How could they truly rejoice that the Long March was over when so many of their comrades were absent? All those who were still with Zhang Guotao—where were they? Where was Zhu De? One of the most beloved members of the army, he was missed more than most. It did not seem right that he was not with them, grinning his perpetual grin, greeting them by name, making jokes.

At the moment, however, they were busy setting up a routine for their new life. The countryside at Wayaobu and at nearby Bao'an (where they moved a few months later) was a jumble of oddly shaped hills that looked as if they had been formed in a hurry and tossed carelessly across the landscape. At first glance there seemed to be no houses, only planted fields, but a closer look showed that the hills had doors. Behind the doors were caves turned into houses. Inside they had whitewashed walls, brick floors, rice-paper windows, and chimneys that erupted from the hillside. The leaders found private caves for themselves, and life began to take on a pattern between morning and evening bugle calls. During the day there was drilling, farming, small industrial ventures, and—most important—schooling.

One morning when Chen Changfeng was bringing Mao his basin of washing water, Mao stopped him. "Chen Changfeng," he said, "I'm sending you to school to study. How do you like that?"

Chen was not sure that he liked it at all. Who would take care of Mao? he wondered. Indeed, how could he let anyone else take care of him? But on the other hand, how could Chen argue with the Chairman? Mao presented him with some pads and pencils and of course Chen went to school. In the end he became an instructor.

Months later when he paid Mao a visit, Mao asked him what kind of instructor he was. "When you're talking," he asked, "do the men stamp their feet and complain about mosquitoes?"

Chen smiled. So Mao knew that when the men stamped their feet during the evening roll-call speech, it was because they were bored! When asked, they would say the mosquitoes were biting.

Chen admitted that sometimes mosquitoes did attend his roll-call lectures. He wasn't a very good speaker yet.

"When you're talking, make things clear," Mao said. "Don't gabble. Don't put on airs."

But it wasn't all work in the army. In the evening bonfires were lit and people sang. There were many Poor Man's Dances and inside the cave houses the men often played cards. Mao Zedong learned to play rummy and solitaire; many played checkers. Often groups would revive the games they had played in Jiangxi. But perhaps one of the happiest occasions in the early months was the day when Liu Ying married Luo Fa, secretary general of the army, the man she'd been working for. Liu Ying said they couldn't afford a wedding or a feast, but Mao insisted they should all have a chance to celebrate and he arranged a reception.

But where was Zhang? Where was Zhu De?

From time to time, coded messages passed between Zhang and Mao, but they were brief, cold, and businesslike. Zhu De was supposed to be commander in chief of the army, yet no word came directly from him. Only much later did they hear about Zhu De and the hardships he had to endure. When Zhang demanded that Zhu De break off his relation with Mao, Zhu refused. How could he deny Mao? he asked. They were one: Zhu-Mao. Then when Zhang ordered him to admit that Mao was wrong about going north, Zhu De again refused. Mao was not wrong, Zhu said.

Zhang tried to force Zhu to change his mind by punishing him. He deprived Zhu of his position as commander in chief. He had Zhu De's horse taken from him and killed. He removed Zhu's security aides and no longer allowed him to see Kang Keqing, who was given the job of rounding up those who lagged behind. Zhu De claimed that such measures were "designed to kill a person without using a knife." Kang Keqing would say later that her time with Zhang Guotao's army was the hardest of the Long March. Still, she and Zhu De were born survivors. It would take more than Zhang Guotao to break their will.

Indeed it was Zhang whose strength would be broken, in one disaster after another. When he found it difficult to feed his troops in Tibetan territory, he told his army that they would go south and capture Chengdu, capital of Sichuan Province. "March to Chengdu and eat rice!" was his slogan but, as it turned out, Chengdu was his first disaster. Chiang Kai-shek sent 200,000 men to Chengdu against Zhang Guotao's 80,000 and in seven days Chiang wiped out 10,000 Red soldiers. By February Zhang had been forced back into Tibetan country with an army of only 40,000, half the number he had started out with. Whether he would admit it or not, he was undoubtedly ready to make some kind of compromise with Mao if he could do it without, as the Chinese say, "losing face."

And he was given an opportunity. A message from Mao reported that an old friend of Zhang's had arrived from Moscow with orders for the Chinese to stop fighting each other and form a united front against Japan. It took a few months for the negotiations to be completed but in the end Zhang agreed to rejoin Mao. In turn, Mao agreed that Zhang could establish his base across the Yellow River north of Mao's army. In the meantime the Fourth Front Army had been joined by the Sixth Army and the Second Army, traveling together. Finally, on July 14, 1936, they all set out and Zhu De was back in command. Kang Keqing was nearby.

One final disaster lay ahead at the Yellow River. Both the Second and Sixth Armies refused to go with Zhang on this last step of his march, although the actual crossing of the river was no problem. Twenty thousand of the Fourth Front (about half) had crossed, when suddenly Nationalists descended in force with a large contingent of Moslem cavalry. What followed was hardly a battle; it was a massacre. The combined Nationalist and Moslem troops slaughtered all 20,000 men on the north bank of the Yellow River and prevented those on the south bank from crossing. Indeed, they pursued some who hadn't crossed, capturing Zhang's entire regiment of 2,000 women.

Only the headquarters unit—Zhang, Zhu De, and others— along with a few thousand troops escaped. They made their way to the town of Huining, where units of the First Front Army awaited them. They celebrated. Those who were alive celebrated simply because they were still alive. They celebrated because they were together. For three nights, October 8 to October 10, they ate their fill of chicken, pork, and mutton while they tried not to think of all those who had not made it.

The official recognition that the various armies were re-united, however, did not take place until December 21, 1936. By this time both the Second and Sixth Armies had arrived, so they were all there—the survivors. They had taken different routes and had arrived at Bao'an at different times but all had made a Long March. All needed a ceremony to mark their endurance against a stubborn enemy and their victory over rivers, mountains, swamps, and miles. More miles than they could have imagined when they started out. Finally they needed to celebrate the settlement of quarrels which had at times threatened their very brotherhood.

The crowd waited around a platform set up across from the Red Army School. Mao Zedong stood in front of the school as Zhang Guotao, Zhu De, and Zhou Enlai rode up to meet him. Everyone cheered as the leaders climbed together onto the platform.

Liu Ying would have been in the audience, stretching to see above the heads of others. Yang Chengwu, his face alight with excitement, would already be filing away the details of this occasion in his memory. Sometimes it must have seemed to him marvelous that he would have such momentous memories to carry through his life. And Chen Changfeng. He would have been filled with pride as Mao Zedong brought the ceremony to a rousing conclusion. Mao was so confident. As modest as his manner was, Mao gave the impression that the future lay in his hands and he knew just what to do with it. At the moment when there was such a high state of unity among them, how could anyone doubt but that one day this unity would take hold over all China? How could anyone doubt but that Mao was right?

AFTER THE LONG MARCH

But Mao was not always right. Men who have the genius to lead revolutions, to inspire people to imagine a new world often do not have the practical skills to govern that world. Mao, however, had thirteen more years before he would be tested.

First Japan had to be defeated and thrown out of China. And the Russians were quite right: The Chinese had to unite. Even the Communists and the Nationalists had to stop fighting each other and join forces to fight their common enemy. And they did. Just a few weeks after the big reunion at Bao'an, a Nationalist officer, who realized that Chiang Kai-shek, stubborn as he was, would never agree to such an alliance unless he was forced, went to Bao'an and offered to help the Communist Army by kidnapping Chiang. As it turned out, Chiang was nearby and it wasn't hard to kidnap him. Although Chiang was furious, in the end he had to agree and the alliance was made.

Japan was not defeated, however, until the whole world was at war and until America had dropped two atom bombs on two Japanese cities in 1945. And then the Nationalists and the Communists had to go back to fighting each other to see who would rule China.

The Communists won the civil war; Chiang Kai-shek and all the Nationalists who could manage to escape went to the island of Taiwan and set up their own government. On October 1, 1949, at an official ceremony in Beijing, Mao Zedong and his leaders officially proclaimed the new government, the People's Republic of China.

It was time for Mao to put his years of dreaming and planning into action. In order to build his new society without interference, he sent foreigners away and killed those enemies who might oppose him. In the privacy of his sealed-off nation he hoped to produce a perfect society. Mao's reforms did change China. Poverty was reduced; property and wealth were redistributed; health was improved; education became widespread. To accomplish this, Mao expected people to abandon old ways for new and put the common good of the country above their personal interests. But this was not always easy, especially when they were supposed to put the country before their families, and forgo private ambitions. In order to survive, Communist governments cannot help but be repressive (some more, some less), and many Chinese, so accustomed to being exploited in the past, expected the government to control their private lives.

The trouble was that as time went on, Mao became impatient. He wanted to make sure that his new world was complete before he died. He worried that people were becoming soft and reverting to old habits. He was afraid that the new generation, which had not experienced a revolution, would not understand the true meaning of this revolution. Just as he'd always believed in hardship, he believed that construction could not take place unless it followed destruction. A new society could be created, he believed, only if like the mythical bird—the phoenix—it rose out of the ashes of its former self.

Mao would no longer listen to the suggestions or criticism of his old comrades. Instead, with the encouragement of his new wife, a jealous, ambitious woman, he began to suspect even his most faithful friends of slipping away from Revolutionary goals. He decided to let members of the new generation create their own revolution and encouraged teenagers known as Red Guards to roam the countryside and destroy remnants of old China and Chinese thought. "Great disorder across the land," Mao wrote, "leads to great order."

And so he sponsored the Cultural Revolution, ten years of chaos, from 1966 to 1976. Schools were closed. Innocent people were humiliated, imprisoned, tortured. Thousands of city people or those who were accused of being intellectuals were sent to the countryside to labor with the peasants and learn from them how to live what Mao believed to be the simple, moral life.

Liu Ying and her husband were put in military custody and sent far away. Yang Chengwu spent seven years in prison. One after another of the Long Marchers was subjected to suspicion and mistreatment. The Red Guards paraded Kang Keqing through the streets as an enemy of Communism. They called Zhu De a "black general" and destroyed the contents of his house. They threw the son of another Long Marcher, Deng Xiaoping, out of a window and crippled him for life. "To think," Zhu De remarked, "that once we all ate out of the same rice bowl."

In 1976 Mao Zedong, Zhu De, and Zhou Enlai died. The Cultural Revolution had petered out and everyone realized that China had lost ten valuable years and would have to begin again. By this time China had opened relations with other countries. Gradually Long Marchers who had suffered in the Cultural Revolution were restored to respectability and often to positions of importance. Deng Xiaoping became the most powerful man in the new government.

Those who are left (about 600) are proud to be survivors of the Long March, proud of their country, but when asked about the Cultural Revolution, they sigh. "Mao made a mistake," they say.

NOTES

Page 13. Once some Red soldiers made what was surely a half-serious scheme to break out of the circle. The scheme had been used in an old story and had worked there. The soldiers lined up fifty water buffaloes in front of some barbed wire connecting the blockhouses. Then they tied firecrackers to the buffaloes' tails and lit them, expecting the animals to charge through the wire just as they had in the story. But the buffaloes hadn't heard that story. Instead, bellowing in anger, they stampeded away, their tails exploding in streams of smoke.

Page 14. An average Chinese farm at this period was 3.3 acres. This yielded about sixteen dollars a year, half of which the landlord took. Peasants were continually forced to borrow from moneylenders who charged thirty-percent interest a year.

Page 16. Mao Zedong was born in Hunan Province on December 26, 1893. His parents were middle-class farmers who were able to see that he was educated, although much of Mao's education was from his own reading. Always a rebel, he believed that the remaking of China had to begin with land reform and a revolution among the peasants.

Otto Braun had been sent from Russia officially as an advisor to China but he presented himself as a leader and the Chinese accepted him as such. On the whole, Russian and Chinese Communists agreed on the principles of revolution: Capitalism (the system of private ownership of property) should be abolished; foreigners should be evicted; class structure should be eliminated from society so workers would run the country. Mao and the Russians disagreed, however, on tactics. The Russians believed that revolution

116

should start with workers in the cities while Mao believed it should start with peasants.

Page 17. A political commissar was an officer in charge of political motivation and the morale of the army. His office was parallel with that of a military commander and he had military responsibilities as well.

Page 20. Japan began its military aggression against Manchuria in 1931.

Page 23. Many Chinese marriages were arranged by the parents of the bride and groom, who often did not even meet until the ceremony.

Page 25. Liu Ying, who had come from an educated family, had been a member of the Communist Party for six years, starting as an underground worker in a city controlled by the Nationalists. Many of her coworkers, including her best friend, had been caught and executed, but Liu Ying was so tiny that she pretended to be a schoolgirl with braids down her back and was never suspected.

Page 26. There is a theory that the vanguard troops made their way easily because of secret agreements with local warlords in control of the area. When the regular Nationalist forces arrived, the battle became serious.

Page 60. This rebellion, known as the Taiping Rebellion, occurred from 1850 to 1865. The execution of the Taiping warriors, in spite of local legend to the contrary, took place for the most part in Chengdu.

Page 113. Zhang Xueliang, known as "The Young Marshal," was Chiang's officer who proposed and arranged the kidnapping. He was later put under house arrest by Chiang and taken to Taiwan.

Page 115. In 1938 Zhang Guotao went over to Chiang Kai-shek's side and he later ended up in exile in Canada.

BIBLIOGRAPHY

WORKS IN ENGLISH

Alley, Rewi. *Land and Folk in Kiangsi: A Chinese Province in 1961*. Peking: New World Press, 1962.

Chen Changfeng. *On the Long March with Chairman Mao*. Peking: Foreign Language Press, 1972.

Chesneaux, Jean, Françoise Le Barbur, and Marie-Claire Bergère. *China: From the 1911 Revolution to Liberation*. New York: Pantheon, 1977.

Clubb, O. Edmund. *Twentieth-Century China*. New York: Columbia University Press, 1964.

Coye, Molly J., Jon Livingston, and Jean Highland (eds.). *China Yesterday and Today* (3rd ed.). New York: Bantam, 1984.

Domes, Jürgen. *Peng Te-huai: The Man and the Image*. Stanford, California: Stanford University Press, 1985.

Fairbanks, John King. *Chinabound: A Fifty-Year Memoir*. New York: Harper & Row, 1982.

Han Suyin. *The Morning Deluge: Mao Tsetung and the Chinese Revolution, 1893–1954*. Boston: Little, Brown, 1972.

Huang Zhen. *Sketches on the Long March*. Beijing, 1982.

Lawrence, Anthony. *China: The Long March*. London: Merehurst Press, 1986.

Liu Po-cheng and others. *Recalling the Long March*. Peking: Foreign Language Press, 1978.

The Long March: Eyewitness Accounts. Peking, 1964.

North, Robert C. *Chinese Communism*. New York: McGraw Hill, 1974.

Payne, Robert. *Mao Tse-Tung*. New York: Weybright and Talley, 1969.

Peng Dehuai. *Memoirs of a Chinese Marshal*. Beijing, 1984.

Roots, John McCook. *Chou: An Informal Biography of China's Legendary Chou En Lai*. New York: Doubleday, 1978.

Salisbury, Charlotte Y. *Long March Diary: China Epic*. New York: Walker, 1986.

Salisbury, Harrison. *The Long March: The Untold Story*. New York: Harper & Row, 1985.

Service, John S. *Lost Chance in China*. New York: Random House, 1974.

Smedley, Agnes. *Battle Hymn of China*. London: Gollancz, 1968.

Smedley, Agnes. *The Great Road*. New York: Monthly Review Press, 1956.

Snow, Edgar. *The Battle for Asia*. New York: Random House, 1941.

Snow, Edgar. *Journey to the Beginning*. New York, 1967.

Snow, Edgar. *Random Notes on Red China*. Cambridge, Massachusetts: Harvard University Press, 1957.

Snow, Edgar. *Red Star over China*. New York: Random House, 1968.

Snow, Helen. *The Chinese Communists*. Westport, Connecticut: Greenwood, 1972.

Snow, Helen Foster. *My China Years: A Memoir*. New York: William Morrow, 1984.

Snow, Helen (Nym Wales). *Red Dust*. Westport, Connecticut: Greenwood, 1972.

Snow, Helen. *Women in Modern China*. The Hague: The Netherlands, 1957.

Spence, Jonathan D. *The Gate of Heavenly Peace: The Chinese and Their Revolution, 1895–1980*. New York: Viking, 1981.

Stories of the Long March. Peking, 1958.

Terrill, Ross. *Mao*. New York: Harper & Row, 1980.

Terrill, Ross. *The White-Boned Demon: A Biography of Madame Mao Zedong*. New York: William Morrow, 1984.

Wei Guolu. *On the Long March as Guard to Chou En-lai*. Peking, 1978.

Wilbur, C. Martin. *The Nationalist Revolution in China, 1923–1928*. Cambridge, England: Cambridge University Press, 1984.

Wilson, Dick. *The Long March*. New York: Viking, 1971.

Wilson, Dick. *Zhou En-lai*. New York: Viking, 1984.

Witke, Roxane. *Comrade Chiang Ch'ing*. Boston: Little, Brown, 1977.

PERIODICALS

Chen Rinong. "Ruijin—Where It Started," *China Reconstructs*, no. 6, May 1984.
Garavente, Anthony. "The Long March," *The China Quarterly*, no. 22, April–June 1965.

WORKS IN CHINESE

Yang Chengwu. *Reminiscences of the Long March (Yi chengzheng).* Beijing, 1982.

PERSONAL INTERVIEWS WITH SURVIVORS OF THE LONG MARCH

Kang Keqing, General Qin Xianghan, Liu Ying, General Yang Chengwu, Ding Ganru, Li Xiauxia, Kong Xianquan, Dai Juming, Shan Guozhen, Tian Xingyong, Li Yang Guan.

INDEX

124